THE LOST BROTHER

ALSO BY RICK BENNET

KING OF A SMALL WORLD

THE LOST BROTHER

RICK BENNET

ARCADE PUBLISHING
NEW YORK

FIRST EDITION

This is a work of fiction. Names, places, characters, and incidents are either the products of the author's imagination or are used fictitiously.

Library of Congress Cataloging-in-Publication Data

Bennet, Rick.
    The lost brother / Rick Bennet/ —1st ed.
        p.   cm.
    ISBN 1-55970-367-9
    I. Title
    PS3552.E54753L67 1996
    813'.54—dc20   96–32789

Published in the United States by Arcade Publishing, Inc., New York

Distributed by Little, Brown and Company

10 9 8 7 6 5 4 3 2 1

Designed by API

BP

PRINTED IN THE UNITED STATES OF AMERICA

THE LOST BROTHER

1

HE'S AN ACTOR, A STREET PERFORMER, this homeless black man in his layers of ragged clothes, with his bearded face and dreadlocked hair, sitting idly on a sidewalk across from the White House. His name is Bobby Jay. He says he's a preacher. Preacher Bobby Jay.

Not too many blocks away, another black man, pudgy, balding, bespectacled Henry James, Washington's top prosecutor, sits on his living room couch, looking out the rain-speckled window to the glistening, shadowed street, grateful for his home's warmth and light, comfortable in his slacks and sweater.

A group of well-dressed Japanese tourists stands before Preacher. Although it's night and they have an almost paranoid fear of America's legendary violence, they think they'll be safe here, so near the President. They see Preacher's cardboard sign, saying: ASK ME ANYTHING FOR I KNOW IT ALL. ONE DOLLAR.

One of the tourists asks if it's true, as he read in the paper back home, that Washington will soon explode in race riots. The Japanese, having some tradition of believing beggars to be wise men, listen sincerely to Preacher's answer.

Henry James's wife, Jessica, joins him on the couch in their comfortable living room. She's his age. White. Blond. Not pretty to most people, but he's not handsome, and neither of them cares much about such things. They met in law school and fell immediately, easily, in love. They communicate without talking; share the same views on issues they argue about.

They have a beautifully refurbished three-story stone row house near Dupont Circle. She has a successful private legal practice; he's *the* Henry James, famous for his extraordinary trial-win percentage. They have two beautiful, healthy, bright children, a twelve-year-old boy, upstairs in his room, and an eight-year-old girl, spending the night with her grandmother, Henry's mother, who lives a short distance but far world from here.

Preacher, for the tourists, waves his arms and twists his body and dances with his words, melodramatic and grandiloquent on his minor stage, the overhead streetlamp for a spotlight, an entertainer in his own way.

"You ask me if the riots are coming? Ask me as well if the *war* is coming. If blacks will get their guns. If whites will. Ask me as well if there is something special happening here, and I say *no!*"

He pauses. Winks. Says, "We've always been this way."

The phone rings. Jessie answers it. It's Henry's mother. She and Jessie talk a few minutes. They get along very well.

Jessie hands the phone to Henry. He hears his daughter on the other end, asking, "Daddy, do I have to go to bed now?"

"When you spend the night with Grandma, you go to sleep when she does."

"But I'm not tired."

"Hon, if you don't go to bed now, your uncle Long is going to get you."

The girl goes quiet.

Jessie *tsk*s at her husband. "You shouldn't do that."

He smiles.

"The kids think Long is the bogeyman," Jessie says.

Henry laughs. He hears his daughter asking her grandmother if it's true that Uncle Long will get her. He hears his mother take the phone and say, "Henry!"

After good nights are said all around and the phone hung up and a minute passes, Jessie asks, "Do you know where he is?"

"Long?" Henry asks, then shakes his head no.

"He's been out a month now?" Jessie asks.

Henry nods. "Mr. Long Ray. Convicted three times for murder but back on the street. I never forget that he's my brother, but he should be locked up for life. He'll kill again, or be killed. It's how he reacts to life's challenges. Three strikes is too many for men like him. Two strikes is."

The Japanese tourists applaud Preacher, amused. They find dollars for him.

Three young black men in low-slung jeans, bulbous jackets, and face-hiding ball caps come up, and the Japanese, having seen such men in rap videos and Hollywood movies, move quickly off.

The first young black man, anger in his eyes, pushes Preacher out of his way. Preacher nods and tries to duck away, but the second young man is behind him now, saying, "What's up, motherfucker? What you doing here? You think that President motherfucker in there, you think he give a *fuck* what you say?"

The third young man, seeing Preacher's sign, kicks it away and says, "Tell me this, know-it-all fool. You so smart, how come you living on the street? Huh?"

Preacher knows better than to talk back to them. He just says, "Okay, okay, uh-huh, uh-huh, that's all right," lowly, to himself, looking down.

The first young man pushes Preacher again. Hard. Preacher falls to the ground. The young men, disgusted, walk on.

It was raining earlier; it rains again now. And though it's April, the temperature drops to close to freezing.

Preacher walks up an alley, debating where to spend the night. He has two regular places: the basement of his recently deceased grandmother's house, where she let him stay when it got cold; and the back-alley sheltered doorway of a restaurant, whose owners feed him sometimes because his presence there prevents burglaries. He prefers the doorway because it's downtown, and his grandmother's house is isolated in a warehouse district a far walk or complicated combination of bus rides from here. He goes to the restaurant now.

When he gets to the doorway, he pulls his blankets from the duffel bag in which he carries his belongings and curls up in them. He's out of the rain but not warm.

Jessie rubs Henry's shoulders. She knows how much stress he's been under. He was publicly adamant about his belief that O. J. Simpson was guilty, and because he was a black man with that view, he got a lot of media attention.

"It's the racial crap that hurts the most," he says bitterly. "Calling me an Uncle Tom because I prosecute black men. What sense does that make? Thirty years ago white juries acquitted whites who killed blacks, and called the prosecutors nigger-lovers. Now it's the other way around."

"A natural swing of the pendulum."

"No. There's no pendulum. There's no excuse."

Jessie keeps rubbing his shoulders. Says, "Shhh." Quick as she is to jump into the intellectual fray with him, she also knows when he's just venting. Lets him.

The doorbell rings. And though their neighborhood is a good one, still, it's the city, it's night.

Henry pulls back the front window curtain. Sees a clean-shaven, short-haired white man at the door, in a suit and tie. If it had been a black male in a hooded sweatshirt, maybe one of those young men who hassled Preacher, Henry might not have opened the door. But it's a suit-and-tie white man, in Washington. Why wouldn't you open the door?

2

CATHERINE "PASSER" JONES SITS at her steel-gray desk in her dismal gray office, exhausted. She was out all night on a surveillance. Witness location. Reluctant witness. Passer had heard of a club this witness frequented. Tailed her to her boyfriend's apartment at four in the morning. Saw the lights go out at five. It's six now.

Passer called and left a message for the client, a lawyer, about where he could find this witness, and then came here to wait for her boss, Kevin Kellogg. He was at a crap game. She paged him. Told him she needed money. Told him to get his ass over here and pay her before he went broke again.

She drinks black coffee. Smokes. Moves to the couch. Lies down. Closes her eyes. Doesn't sleep.

She's twenty-four. She shares an apartment with an accountant, a woman, who shops, cooks, cleans, dates, remembers birthdays, and works regular hours. Passer does none of those things. Passer works a lot, writes a little, exercises some, and sleeps when she gets the chance. She's been working as an operative under Kellogg's private investigator license for two years. She loves the job when she doesn't hate it. Stretched out now on the tattered brownish office couch, she hates it. She's dressed in black boots, blue jeans, black windbreaker with shoulder pads, and an Orioles ball cap; she keeps her hair cut short so that anyone walking past as she sits in a car overnight thinks she's a man, not a victim. Spending the night in a car, pissing into a bedpan with a newspaper on her lap, isn't as thrilling as it used to be, but it's her life, and she's taking it for a while.

The office door opens. Kevin Kellogg comes in, with his secretary, Sue Cline, right behind. Kellogg is fifty years old. Medium height, grossly overweight, blotchy white skin, thinning white hair. He's dressed in billowing black pants held up by black suspenders; rumpled white shirt unbuttoned at the top; loose red tie; scuffed, never polished black shoes. Dressed as he always is. Every day, work or not. In a courtroom, at the racetrack, hearing a client, shooting dice, it's all the same to him. He's single. Never married. Lives in a downtown hotel. Owns a closet and dresser of clothes; this business and its equipment and furniture; an old Pontiac that used to be a taxi and still looks like one; nothing else.

Sue Cline is a short, plain woman in her thirties. Wal-Mart shopper, wearer. Uneducated formally or otherwise. A natural redhead from West Virginia, hired because when she borrowed money from Kellogg at the track and promised to pay him back the next day, she'd driven a hundred miles through a snowstorm to do it.

Kellogg's grumpy. Doesn't look at Passer as she sits up.
Passer shakes her head, ready to be angry.

"I don't want to hear your shit, Kevin," she says.

"Shut up."

"You shut up. Asshole." She rubs her eyes.

"Don't worry, Pass," Sue says. "We're all right."

"Were you with him?"

"Yeah. The stakes were too small for him to lose it all.
Black Television Network paid us cash for the Ottaway case.
Four thousand."

Passer stands, relieved. "BTN paid us cash? Tell me
you're going to settle me up?"

Sue nods. Reaches into her purse. Takes out an enve-
lope. Says, "I saved three hundred off the top—Kevin, are
you listening?"

He grunts.

"I saved three hundred off the top to clear our tab with
the Koreans."

The Korean owners of the twenty-four-hour coffee
shop on this building's street level let them run a tab, which
Kellogg covers. It's the staff's perk. Their second office.

Sue continues, "And I took eighteen hundred for the
rent, last month's and next's."

"That's got to come from legal income," Kellogg says.
"If we have cash receipts from the landlord, then we have
to admit we paid him cash, which means we have to admit
we got paid cash or have a cash withdrawal of that much,
which we don't have, which means we'd have to pay taxes
on it."

"I understand that better than you," Sue says testily.

"But since we don't have enough in the bank to pay the rent, what am I supposed to do?"

"We're collecting from Barneson and Row this week. That'll cover it."

Sue isn't convinced but lets it go. "Make sure BTN knows not to file anything with our name on it," she says.

"They know, they know. They don't want any record of this, either. That's why they paid us this way."

"Can you take care of the in-house shit later?" Passer asks.

"Sure," Sue says sympathetically. "You got seventeen hundred coming, right?"

Passer nods.

"What?" Kellogg says, incredulous. "That can't be right."

"I haven't been paid in three weeks, Kevin," Passer says. "And I'm in no mood for bullshit."

"She has to be paid on the books," Kellogg says.

Passer is ready to explode. "If the client is off the books, then so is my pay!"

"Pass," Sue says, "you billed five-forty on that case. That much I'll give you cash for. The rest I'll also give you cash for, but you'll have to sign a check back to us later and pay us the deductions then."

"Fine, fine," Passer says.

Sue counts out her money. Hands it over. Passer takes it. Leaves. Bangs the door behind her as she does.

Kellogg shrugs. "She acts like she's the one who bet the don't against eight straight passes."

"Really," Sue says. "Imagine expecting to get paid on time. The nerve of some people."

"Heh, heh, heh," Kellogg says, mocking laughter. "Heh, heh, heh, heh, heh."

"Shut up, Kevin."

He laughs for real.

Kellogg goes into his windowless, chipping-green-painted, industrial-carpeted office. Sits in his comfortable chair at his broad desk, cluttered, as is the whole room, with equipment. He does most of his work here, at his desk. Using his computer, his phone, his fax.

He's not going to sleep this morning, so he drinks from his coffeepot. Straight from it. He's put masking tape on its lip so as not to burn himself. He drinks two, three, four pots a day. Smokes that many packs of cigarettes. Eats bacon, ham, eggs, and pancakes for breakfast, hamburgers and fries for lunch, steak or fried chicken for dinner. Doughnuts with the breakfast, ice cream with the lunch, cake with the dinner. Pie late at night. Candy bars anytime.

He drinks from the pot, sets it down. Lights a cigarette. Rolls, in his chair, to the cabinet with the Ottaway file. Pulls it. Looks at it. Thinks about it.

The woman he dealt with at Black Television Network asked him if it wouldn't make sense for him to get rid of any evidence that he'd taken the job, in case the IRS looked into it.

There's a set of still photos of the target, Michael Ottaway, with Passer at a bar. Passer was using the name "Sheila." She was made up, and dressed and acted, like a light-skinned black girl for the part. They got photos of her looking scared and intimidated at the bar as Ottaway leered at her. More damaging than the photos, though, are the cassette tapes of the phone calls.

Kellogg plays the best tape.

He hears Passer's voice say, sleepily, "Hello?"

Ottaway, husky-voiced: Hey, baby.

Passer: Oh, you're finally calling me? I thought you said we were going to a party last night.

Ottaway: We are, baby. It's starting right now.

Passer: What kind of a party starts at . . . two in the morning?

Ottaway: The best kind. My kind. Private kind.

Passer: You're supposed to be Michael Ottaway, executive producer, not Michael Ottaway, party thrower. (She was careful to work his full name into the conversation.)

Ottaway: I keep telling you, this is the entertainment business. Now it's time you started entertaining me.

Passer: Let's be professional about this. You keep saying I'll get that job, but it doesn't happen.

Ottaway: You got to understand, if you want me to do for you, you have to do for me.

Passer, after hesitating: Mr. Ottaway, if I come over there . . . do I get the job?

Ottaway: Yeah, baby. You just got to handle this little audition.

Kellogg hears the urgency in Ottaway's voice. He shakes his head, embarrassed for the man, disgusted by him. Passer said later she couldn't believe how blind Ottaway was. She was worried, at the time, about being too obvious.

Kellogg lies down on the couch. Nods off. Gets woken by Sue Cline a few hours later.

He looks at his watch and sees it's not time for his meeting. Looks at her face and sees there's something else.

She points to the television. News report.

Henry and Jessica James were found murdered this morning.

3

A BLACK POLICE OFFICER COMES DOWN the front steps of the James house. His longtime partner, a white man, is leaning back against their patrol car, looking up at the overcast early-morning sky.

"They're not letting anyone in," the black officer says.

"They're paranoid. Look how many press dogs are already here."

"I got the scoop, though. Decapitated, both of them."

"No fuck! You see the bodies?"

"Wouldn't let me in for that. But I talked to Johnson—she's first officer—and she told me."

"What she say?"

The black officer laughs. "Okay, check this out. She gets the call, with her partner. They go in and they see a blood trail, like the garbage man that called this in saw through the back door, which was open. So, you know, they got their guns up, and they go in through the kitchen, and in the living room they see the bodies. The partner, he goes on upstairs, you know, looking to see if the perp's still here, while Johnson, she goes to check the bodies for life. Now, you know, she sees the blood, all this ton of blood, but still she's got to check for life, you never know. But she's also got her gun out and she's looking around because the premises isn't secured yet, so she's really only looking at the bodies out of the corner of her eye. She puts her hand on the woman's neck, wanting to feel body temperature or a pulse or something, and the fucking *head* falls off!"

Both officers crack up, laughing.

Hank Thomas is called the Black Detective. He was first promoted into an office that already had a detective named Thomas, a white man, and so callers forgetting his first name, when asked which Thomas they wanted, sometimes referred to him as the black one, the black detective (there weren't many black detectives at all then). The white detectives had been happy to call him "the black one." Now everyone does.

He looks around the Jameses' living room. Not at the dead bodies. At the live ones. The lieutenant, the captain, the two assholes from the Chief's office, who are really from the Mayor's office. The lab techs. The MEs.

He sighs. As the primary investigator on this homicide, he theoretically could get them out of here, but that's on the same page as the one that says a detective will be judged only by the quality of his work.

His lieutenant comes up. A reasonable man. White man.

"At least it's indoors," the lieutenant says, commiserating. "At least the press isn't videotaping all this shit like they did with the Simpson scene, so they can nitpick us in court. We got uniforms outside keeping them back, and the rest of the homicide squad out canvassing. Hopefully we can get neighbors before they leave for work."

The Black Detective nods. Looks around. Sees what he presumes is the Jameses' video camera. It's on. He makes a note to check the tape.

He looks at the walls. Covered with blood. The letters *LTC* have been painted on in wide swaths.

"What's LTC?" someone asks.

"League of True Colors," someone answers. "White supremacist group."

They hear a pop. Another. A third. Gunshots, from outside the house. Distant.

Homicide detective John Mallory, fifty, dark-haired, well tanned, handsome in a slick way, fit, not too tall, steps out of an alley, hands up, badge in one hand, gun in the other, signaling to the uniforms rushing over that it's okay, don't shoot, put your guns away, God damn it.

Report: A block and a half off, checking an alley, a Dumpster. Sees a suit jacket covered with blood. Hears a noise. Turns. Sees a white man in pants that match the bloody jacket. The man's shirt is bloody. The man is nervous. Mallory pulls his gun. The man pulls one too. Mallory shoots, three times because the man didn't seem fazed by the first hit.

Woman Host: Well, good afternoon, brothers and sisters, good afternoon. Welcome to Black Talk Radio. Let's get right into it. Hello?

Caller: Hello?

Host: What's the word, brother?

Caller: I want to talk about that James murder.

Host: For the people who haven't heard yet, Henry James and his white—excuse me, slip of the tongue there, like *fag* for Frank—Henry James and his *wife* were found murdered this morning.

Caller: You know what the word on the street is?

Host: You're the street. This is the wire. Put it out.

Caller: That's his punishment.

Host: How do you mean?

Caller: That's his punishment because Whitey lost the Simpson case, and they mad. They mad at all these house-nigger prosecutors they got.

Host: But he's not the one who lost that case.

Caller: No, no, he didn't lose the case personally, but I'm saying The Man is pissed off, so he whacked Henry James as a lesson to all the other black prosecutors. The Man set it all up on O.J., all that fake evidence and all, but the good people on the jury saw through it, and so The Man is all mad.

Host: That's a point, that's a point.

Caller: You understand what I'm saying? And I don't even care. I got no sympathy for Henry James, marrying a white woman and working against his own kind.

Host: Well, I don't know I go that far. He was still a black man, our brother, and even if he was a lost brother, we all end up in the same black heaven with our African Father of All and our Lord Black Jesus.

Next caller, you're on the air, Black Talk Radio.

Second Caller: I want to say, that James murder, it got to

be a fix. That white detective, Mallory, he's been caught before fixing things, and here he is again, this time killing the man who *supposedly* killed Henry James. How we know that man did it? Dead now!

Host: Ain't that something, sister?

Caller: I mean, I'm sorry the people got killed, even if Henry James was an Uncle Tomfool. But you *know* it's the devil's work and they going to say there's blood evidence. I say that's all DNA voodoo.

Host: That's fresh. DNA voodoo.

Caller: You understand what I'm saying? They call our traditional science voodoo, so I call *their* science voodoo. You know those forensic scientists say whatever the police tell them to say. They all lie. Try to say there's DNA evidence against O.J., or proof that we genetically less intelligent. Don't none of it mean nothing, because those scientists, they just find what they told to find. They all lie. They all a bunch of Mark Fuhrmans.

Host: I'm okay with that, thank you. Next caller, you're on the air.

Third Caller: Sister, how you?

Host: Talk to me, fine woman.

Caller: I want to say, first, to all the brothers out there, you know we love you.

Host: We do, we do.

Caller: But you all keep messing with white women, you got to *know* what it leads to.

Host: Tell it, sister.

Caller: You got the finest women in the world, but you let yourselves wander right into the devil's trap.

Host: Ain't no one here going to argue with you.

Caller: But I got to say, I don't care about Henry James or his wife.

Host: Oh, sister, you have to find it in you.

Caller: No, because they gone. My concern is with the living. I'm talking about the boy.

Host: Yes! Let me tell the listeners who might not know, but the Jameses got two children, and the little boy is missing. The girl spent the night with her black grandmother, so she's all right, and we appreciate the symbolism of *that*. But her brother was home, and he is gone, and God knows what happened to him.

4

A BLACK MAN, SITTING ON THE BED in a cheap hotel room, intently watches a news show on television:

Host: We're here with Mr. Jimmy Close of the League of True Colors. Mr. Close, the alleged killer of Henry and Jessica James has now been identified as a Richard Ells, most recently of Charles Town, West Virginia. Your headquarters are located just a few miles from there, in Harpers Ferry, and as you know, Ells used the victims' blood to paint the letters *LTC* on the walls. Yet you deny any connection with Mr. Ells.

Close: We have checked our records, which are computerized, and found that his sole connection to us was that he attended one of our meetings, where he signed the guest sheet.

Host: But he had LTC literature in his pockets.

Close: He probably picked it up at that meeting.

Host: It isn't this show's purpose or ability to investigate the depth of your connection with Richard Ells. We're here to ask you whether there isn't at least a philosophical connection.

Close: None.

Host: No connection between a philosophy of racial hate and the murder of an interracial couple?

The black man in the hotel room turns off the set. Lies back on the bed, his hair grazing the headboard, his feet hanging over the other end. He's six feet ten. When he gets up from chairs, he seems more to unfold than rise; when he walks down streets, more to flow than step. He is slender but clearly strong; his forearms ripple at slight movements. His deep-furrowed eyes seem always to be glowering, and it has been true of his life that, without trying, he intimidates. It has also been true of his life that he has often deliberately intimidated. It is true that even as a child he found he could get things from people by pressing their fear of him. And it is true, he thinks now, that he was thus seduced into that part of the world where the fear he inspires is an asset, not a handicap. Drawn into that part of the world because to belong to the broader world meant a constant effort to dispel fears, a constant effort to prove himself "safe," a constant effort to apologize for what he was born to look like. And it is true that once he set down that other road, there was no turning back. As a teenager stealing cars, dealing drugs, robbing dealers, and finally killing in what was effectively, if not legally, self-defense, he earned himself a sheet and a rep.

His mother, good woman, English teacher, taught him to read and write, to appreciate literature, to speak clearly if he wanted. His stepfather, good man, was too late and too different to teach him manhood. His natural father, Raymond Ray, Ray Ray, was a small-time hustler, numbers runner, and pimp, whose sole act of fatherhood after conception was to look at the baby and pronounce him long. Long. Long Ray.

Long now is in this room in this downtown hotel. He's spent the last sixteen years in prison; he has spent much of the month since his release in this room, carefully working his way back into the world. He reads. Goes to McDonald's. Watches television. Goes to the movies. He's afraid to do much more. If he goes for a walk in the city, old friends might see him, buy him drinks, get him high, suck him in; old vendettas could flame. But if he goes outside the city he'll be a giant, harsh-looking black man with a record, walking around a white suburb, having to convince the cops who'll find a pretense for stopping him that he's just out for a stroll. He wouldn't believe him if he were them.

He takes a shower. Sits under the water for forty-five minutes, appreciating the freedom to do that.

Then, still naked, he sits by the window overlooking the busy afternoon street, watching the people. He's fascinated by the variety. By the presence of women and children. By the freedom. But how do they stay free? How do they not find themselves tested, pushed, trapped, threatened into violence?

But he doesn't blame anyone else for his own life. He doesn't blame society, or his absent natural father, or whites, or God. He sees life as a tree and all the differences between us as branches splitting off until you end up with people as leaves, some of which get a lot more light than others.

If you asked him what he is, where someone else might say sales clerk or carpenter or engineer, Long would say motherfucker. What are you? I'm a motherfucker. What are you good at? Being a motherfucker. Tell me, what is it good for? Absolutely nothing. Who do you blame? No one. What do you want? To stay out of prison. To not have to work at a teenager's job. If someone were to describe you in one word, what would it be?

He dresses. Blue jeans, black sneakers, yellow sweatshirt.

He goes out. Down to the Mall, to watch the sky change colors as the sun sets. He listens to music through headphones, which is how convicts are used to listening to it.

The sun goes down and he stands up, heads off, walking because he knows it's useless for a man who looks like him to flag a cab. Even the black drivers won't stop for him. He wouldn't stop, either, if he were them.

Moving through the city, he's haunted by the life he might have had. He sees it in a woman's kind eyes, in the gentle smile of a father out with his children. He's seen it on television, read about it in books, thought about it in bed. He doesn't cry about it anymore. That wouldn't do any good. It wasn't meant to be.

He stops to eat at a steak house, where first the young black hostess and then the gay white waiter eye him suspiciously, force pleasant, cold politeness into their voices. Seated in the back, he sets a hundred-dollar bill on the table to calm them down. Orders his steak and fries and salad and dessert. Takes his time eating, wanting to enjoy the taste. He read once about how waiters, white and black both, didn't like serving black customers because they didn't tip. Long became furious when he read that. But that was then. Now he tries—his release resolution—to see himself through the world's eyes. Here, through the eyes of a waiter who works for tips but finds one type of person consistently underpaying him; of a hostess who maybe has been abused by a man as fierce as Long looks to be. He counsels himself to feel what it's like to deal with someone—him—who could kill you with his bare hands. Or rape you or rob you or beat you. Someone who can be counted on to refrain from taking what he wants from you only by laws and guns. That most brutal of realities dominates his relations with the world: he can take what he wants, and the world knows it. That those with physical power may abuse it is the most primal of human fears, of human evils. Power sometimes corrupts. Physical power sometimes physically corrupts. Long has sometimes been corrupted.

He finishes eating. Pays. Tips. Finishes the walk to his destination, his mother's house. There, he looks around. This is a marginal neighborhood, but it's not the criminals he fears; it's the police or the press. He walks down the street, staying in the shadows as best he can. Checking the parked cars. He sees no one. So he walks back up the street and at his mother's row house takes the three steps to her porch in a single bound.

The first floor is dark, but there's a light on upstairs. He rings the bell. Hears the second-floor window open. Sees his mother's head lean out. Steps back so she can see it's him. She does. She shakes her head, stunned. Ducks back in. A moment later the door opens. He moves quickly inside. She shuts the door behind him, and they hug, he stooping way down to take her in his arms.

They move through the dark living room, seeing by the light of the bulb at the top of the stairs. They sit on the couch. He peers out the front window, checking the street.

He pulls the curtain tight. Turns on a table lamp. Looks at his mother as she looks at him.

"Henry told me you got out a month ago," she says.

"I guess he'd know." Long hesitates. Says, "I'm sorry, Mama."

"It's okay. I know you got to do things in your own time, your own way."

"No, I mean about Henry."

She takes a deep breath. A tear falls down her tired face. She nods. "Is that what brought you by?"

"Yes."

"And you wouldn't have come otherwise?"

He shrugs that he doesn't know.

"Are you sorry for Henry or for me?" she asks.

"You."

"And no part of you is sorry for him? Or Jessica?"

"I never met her. I never understood him."

That's not true. Long had understood Henry. Henry the bookworm boy. Henry the can't-run-or-jump boy. Henry the don't-call-them-spics/kikes/faggots/bitches/honkies boy. He had understood Henry.

"He didn't hate you," his mother says.

"I didn't hate him. We just didn't have anything to talk about."

"You know he was behind the library expansion down there?"

"Yeah?"

"I think he thought it was the one thing he could do for you."

"Good thing he didn't try anything else. He put away half the guys on my cell block. That's why I couldn't let you visit or call. You've gone to so many of his trials, sitting there so proud of him, that everybody knows you. Good thing he took your husband's name and not our father's."

Her husband, Long and Henry's stepfather, moved them to D.C. from East Saint Louis when Henry was ten and Long sixteen. He found work at the Bureau of Engraving and Printing, she taught in the public schools. Henry took the stepfather's name. Long did not. Long got arrested his first week in the city because, as a new kid, he hadn't dared say no to the idea of stealing a car when the local corner boys had asked him along. He was released and arrested again two days later, then sent to reform school, and upon release from there lived on his own, unable to get along with a stepfather who insisted he live right or get out.

Mrs. James sighs from deep within herself. Long takes her hand. "His death hurts you, and I'm sorry for that. Are you mad? Mad it wasn't me?"

"No."

"It should have been. I've been shot twice and shanked three times. I've done every drug you can think of and had sex with the most disease-ridden women you can imagine. But here I am."

"Thank God," she says.

"God's got nothing to do with my life."

Mrs. James is a churchgoer, but she lets Long's statement go.

A shadow moves over them. Long looks up. Sees a child peering out at him from between the rails, framed by the light at the top of the stairs.

"Come here, girl," Mrs. James says.

The girl comes down.

"You're my uncle Long?" she asks, disbelieving, eyes wide.

"Yeah," Long answers, nervously. He isn't comfortable around children. He hasn't known any since he was himself one, and they seem foreign to him. Especially a beautiful girl like this.

"Are you going to eat me?" she asks him.

He laughs at her seriousness. Says, "No."

"An uncle is a father's brother," she says. "And the daughter of the father is the uncle's niece."

"That's right."

"Are you a bad man?"

"Yes."

"My mommy said you weren't really bad, just got in trouble once and couldn't get out of it."

"She said that?"

"She said that's why it's important not to get in trouble to begin with."

"She's right."

"She said that you had to be some good, though, because once, when my daddy was little, some big kids were hitting him and you came running over and beat them up, and there was a hundred of them!"

Long smiles at the memory. "Five of them. Anacostia boys."

"So then you're really good!" the girl says.

She moves to stand very close to him. He looks back at her, appreciating how fragile the world must seem to her now. He tries his best to soften his face.

She looks from him to her grandmother and back again,

and back again. Then she jumps into her grandmother's hugging arms, crying, saying she wants Mommy and Daddy. Mrs. James rocks her, tells her they're in heaven, she misses them too, but they're with God in heaven.

Long has seen a lot of violence but rarely cared about it. He's committed violence; suffered it. Not often thought about it as right or wrong, only as being. Often it's been fun, exciting. That's what the citizens don't understand about the street. The excitement of crime and chase. The drama.

He looks at this girl crushed by her losses, and part of him, bitterly, thinks, So what, she's crying like a baby, like a spoiled child who thought—what?—that it couldn't happen to her? That she was somehow special and protected? That she was better than him?

But also, part of him sees only a child, maybe one he'd not have been so different from, if he'd grown up in different circumstances; a child hurt as he himself was, even if he never admitted as much.

He reaches out. Puts his tremendous hand on her shoulder.

She turns. Looks at him. Stops crying.

For the first time in his life, he recognizes the face of innocence when he sees it.

She says, "I even wish my brother was here. Even if he's mean to me, I wouldn't care. I just wish he was here."

Long nods.

"Will you find him for me? Hey, Grandmommy, maybe Uncle Long can find him! You said the police might be bad, so maybe Uncle Long can find him!"

Mrs. James says, softly, Maybe.

Long looks at her. At his mother. At the pictures of Henry and Jessica on the end table.

Mrs. James takes the girl back to her room, puts her to sleep. Long looks around his mother's living room while she's gone. At the knickknacks. The nice, well-kept furniture. The painting of a white Jesus. The photos of family. None of Long. He told her to take them down because he didn't want anyone who visited her to find out Henry had a brother and start asking questions. Long told her to take his pictures down, to not visit or call him in jail or prison, to not come to his trials. He wanted her to forget him. Bad enough he hurt himself.

He looks around the room and thinks for the millionth time how different his life is from everyone else's, in the little ways, in the physical objects surrounding them.

His mother returns; invites him into the kitchen for tea. They sit there a moment before Long asks, "What's going on with the boy?"

"I don't know. The police were here for hours, asking questions."

"What did you say to them?"

"There's nothing I can tell them. I don't know anything. I don't even know if I can trust them. I know Henry didn't."

"Mr. Law Enforcement himself didn't trust the police?"

"Not since the Mayor got reelected. I think Henry was handling a real big corruption investigation into the Mayor's office and the police and all."

"Ain't no shortage of shit in this city. Was he working with the FBI?"

"Was Henry? You know, he didn't talk to me much

about these things, but once in a while he'd say some little thing. I remember him once saying that the Mayor was a thief and had the police in his pocket, and when I said I bet the FBI was looking into it, Henry got a funny look on his face and got real quiet."

She sets a cup of tea on the kitchen table in front of Long. Sits across from him, not drinking anything herself. Long sips from his cup. She cries silently.

"I can't sleep," she says. "Can't eat. Knowing that boy might be out there somewhere. Dear God."

"They got the guy who killed Henry."

"Yes. They say so."

"Is there anyplace the boy might go besides here?"

"No. That's why I'm so scared. He knows how to get here. It's only a mile. If he didn't come here, and he wasn't at the house, and if the killer didn't take him, then I don't understand what could have happened."

"Is there a friend or someone he might have gone to?"

"No. The police have questioned all his classmates and friends."

"And they've searched the neighborhood. I saw that on television."

"We had the whole congregation out looking too."

Long shakes his head. He wants to give her hope. But he has none himself.

"The one thing I can think of," she says, "that I didn't tell the police, because it didn't come to me then, the one name, is a man called Chavez. Arcides Chavez."

"Spanish?"

"From El Salvador."

"All the same to me."

"This man, his wife got raped and killed last year, and Henry prosecuted the case. Lost. He almost cried about losing that case, the evidence was so clear. But you know how things are with city juries. That's been going on a long time now, even if it wasn't publicized before O.J. Anyway, when the defendants heard they were free, oh, they high-fived and cheered and laughed. One of them looked Chavez in the eye, grabbed his crotch and licked his lips. But Chavez, I remember watching his face when the verdict was read. Chavez, he had pride. And he told Henry thank you. Henry was saying how sorry he was, but Chavez said it was okay, thank you, you are a good man. Then, later, Chavez had something to do with Henry. I don't know what. The boy told me, one night when he and his sister were sleeping over, that Chavez was working for Henry, or doing something. And I remembered this afternoon, because I was thinking about everything, that the boy said Chavez wasn't afraid of anything. I think he said that Henry said Chavez was a hero, or people like Chavez are heroes. And he also said something about going to Chavez, or calling Chavez, or something, if he got in trouble."

"You didn't tell the police this?"

"No, I don't know that it's important, although just now, talking about it, I think more of it. Maybe I should call the police back? But you know, Chavez, he hated the police in this city. I mean, really hated them. And somehow I think there might be a connection between whatever it was he was doing for Henry and the police. It's probably nothing. I don't know how it could be something. I wish I could remember exactly what the boy said. Do you think you could ask around?"

"I'm going to tell you the truth, Mama. I don't think there's any chance the boy's alive. If he just ran away, just escaped, he would have turned up, he'd have no reason not to. And he can't be hiding. The whole city is looking for him. Somebody got him, and it couldn't have been anyone good."

"But maybe he's afraid. He's a smart boy, and if he's afraid of the police, then he won't come here."

Long sighs. In his heart he knows the boy has to be dead. Long knows too much about criminal realities to believe otherwise.

He says, "I'll go on the street. I'll ask around about what might be up. I'll even call the Mayor."

"Did you meet him in prison?"

Long laughs. "Mama, I ran that joint. He's the mayor out here, but I was the mayor in there. He owes me. And I'll get the New Africa people on the job too. You know who Khalid is?"

Her face tightens. Long realizes the error in mentioning Khalid, because Khalid has long been Henry's most vocal critic.

"You know him?" she asks angrily.

"Forget it. Anyway, about Chavez, I don't know. I'll try to find him, but I don't know any of those people. And remember, it was only a few years ago that they threw that riot against 'our' police."

5

AN OLD BLACK MAN IN A CHEAP SUIT stands at the microphone, peering out into the dark room at the smoke-hidden
customers. Without particular enthusiasm, he introduces
the jazz quartet behind him. Without particular enthusiasm,
the club's customers clap. Without particular enthusiasm,
the bass and the drums start in, and the keyboards tinkle a
slight contribution. But the boy on the tenor sax, he ignores
everyone else's jaded hindsight and lets loose, lost in a
dreamy-dream future of Harlem and Chicago and L.A. gigs.
He stays in that dreamland for two minutes, three minutes,
four and five and six minutes, and by seven the vets have
picked things up, the customers are tapping their feet and
nodding their heads, and Kevin Kellogg, way in the back,
drinking his whiskey, smoking his Kools, smiles, eyes closed,
grateful for the minor miracle of a heartfelt wail.

It's DeJazBa. Thirty-three years on U Street, through
all that thin to find itself finally tasting some thick again as

the neighborhood bounces back. Kellogg looks around and for the first time in a long time sees he's not the only white customer. Isn't sure he likes that.

He listens to Kid Horn; stares into his whiskey. Sips the last of it. Stares into the empty glass. Jerks his head off its drunken doze to call for the waitress but finds she's already there, setting his next shot on the table.

He thinks about things—what drunk doesn't; remembers things—what drunk doesn't; remembers a waitress he had here two years ago. She came up to his table that afternoon. He ordered his whiskey straight up then too.

"I heard about you," she said.

"What?"

"The last man in America drinking whiskey like that."

"The last one not on skid row anyway."

She went off to get his drink. He checked her out. She was a tough make: part black, part white. Some Mex, maybe. Some Asian.

She came back. Put the glass on his table.

"What all are you?" he asked.

She stared at him. She'd heard the question too many times not to be annoyed by it. Said, in perfect TV-white English, "What do you think I am?"

"You can't work here if you're not black."

She said, in exaggerated city-black accent, "Dat a fac, ofay-pattay?"

"I'm not Irish."

In a perfect Irish accent, she said, "Ay, me mother in Dublin would cry if I could not tell that."

He laughed.

She didn't.

"Where you from?" he asked.

"L.A."

"Where in L.A.?"

"Hollywood."

"You grew up there?"

"People do."

"It's a tough neighborhood."

"Yep."

"You got some Mex in you?"

"Sí Señor Vendejo. Soy Mexicana. Por qué?"

"Nothing. Calm down."

Back to a street black's voice, she said, "Motherfucker, don't be telling *me* to calm down. I be as mad as I wanna be, you know what I'm saying? I'll fuck your white ass *up*."

He smiled. "How long you been in Washington?"

Only because it was her first night on the job and she didn't want to offend a regular customer, she sighed and answered, instead of shrugging and walking off. "Three weeks."

"What brings you here?"

"A guy I met in New Orleans. From here. When he wanted to come back here, I came along. Hadn't been east before."

"You with the guy now?"

"No. He was an excuse, not a reason."

"I understand."

"Shit you do."

"You'd be surprised."

"I would."

"And what do you want to be when you grow up?" he asked.

She looked around the room, hoping to see another customer needing attention. But there were only a few people in the club that early that night, and the other waitress had them. "A writer," she said, not really wanting to tell him or anyone else that, but not wanting him or anyone else to make her lie, either.

"Oh, yeah? Ever read Raymond Chandler?" Kellogg asked. "He lived in L.A."

"Ever read Dashiell Hammett? He was born in Maryland."

"You've read Hammett?"

"Yas, suh. I be an ed-chu-cated nee-gro."

"But you're working in a dump like this."

"And you're drinking in it."

"I'm a dump kind of guy."

"I can see that."

"You know, I could use someone like you."

"For what?"

"Why do you think I asked you about Chandler?"

"What, you're a private investigator?"

He nodded.

She laughed.

"What's your name?" he asked.

"If you're any good, you can find that out on your own. And if you aren't any good, why would I want to work for you?"

"I'll give you a call."

"Sure."

"And when I do, I'm going to ask for someone named Passer."

"Why?"

"Because if you ain't that, you're not what I need."

She stared at him. Took him in. Said, "Think I haven't been called that before?"

And now, on this April night two years later, Catherine "Passer" Jones is taking a seat next to him.

"You found me," Kellogg says, loudly. "You ace skip tracer, you."

"Shut up, Kevin."

"You drinking?"

"I'm here on business."

"Great," he says.

"We got a customer."

"Great. You drinking?"

She sighs. Concedes. Kellogg waves to the waitress, who motions to the bartender, who pours two whiskeys, one straight up for him, one on the rocks with soda and two cherries for Passer, both of which the waitress, a black woman Kellogg's age and mind-set, brings over and sets down.

Kellogg lights two cigarettes. Gives one to Passer, which she takes and drags deeply from before sipping.

"You hate it here, don't you?" he asks.

"Don't start on that again."

"But you do. You hate places like this."

"I worked here, remember?"

"For three nights."

"Still, I worked here."

"Slumming. Still are."

"Okay."

"That kid's got a special horn."

"He is good."

"I sit here two, three nights a week, getting shit-faced, hearing dead-end jazz, just hoping that once in a while I'll hear something special."

"You get drunk here because it's walking distance from that thing you call an apartment and you can't afford another DWI."

"That, too."

"I just talked to Sue. She said a man named Jimmy Close called."

"I know that name."

"Founder and president of the League of True Colors."

"Yeah."

"He's looking for a private investigator. Told Sue he's been turned down by the first six places he called."

Kellogg laughs. "Gee, I wonder why that might be."

"Well, like you like to say, private investigators should be dicks, not pussies."

"Actually, what I say is that people should have genitals and not be them."

"Okay. Anyway, Sue said he sounded desperate. And she's from West Virginia, and he is, and LTC started there, and so she wants you to take him on."

"Shit, take him on and the whole city will close down on me. Fair or not, the press has demonized the man. Blacks in this town think he's Hitler come home."

"So where does that leave us?"

Kellogg stares down into his glass, which is empty again. A sick smile comes to his face. "Call him. Now. Tell him to meet us at the office. No, downstairs, at the diner. I'm hungry."

She gets up. Walks to the pay phone back by the rest rooms. Every man in the joint watches her.

Kellogg takes a deep breath, slowly lets it out. Stares up at the ceiling. Down at the floor. At the customers, the employees, the tables, the bottles behind the bar. Thinks, Yeah, I'll take on Mr. Jimmy Close. Why not? Kellogg Investigations. Known throughout the city as the place to go for the street work. The pimp, dealer, gambler work. The after-hours, gutter-time, downside work. Kevin Kellogg. King of shit hill. Fuck my drunk white ass.

6

ONE IN THE MORNING.

Kellogg and Passer, he in his black slacks and white shirt and loose red tie, and she in her black jeans, sneakers, and windbreaker, drink coffee, wait. They look out the window at the empty, steel-and-glass-office-lined downtown street, headlight lit and oil rainbowed; look at the few other customers and the diner employees, all tired, slumping, downward-gazing, up too late.

Kellogg chain-smokes. Passer occasionally smokes. They don't talk much but don't feel uncomfortable in the silence. He told her long ago that they'd go nuts trying to fill their time together with conversation, so just shut up and daydream. Listen to the jazz on the radio.

A taxi pulls up outside, and Kellogg and Passer watch the middle-aged white male passenger pay the driver, get out, come in.

"Yo," Kellogg calls out with a wave as Close enters. Close comes to their booth.

"Mr. Kellogg?" he says.

"Come on, man, who else is going to call you over?" Kellogg says, looking annoyed.

"Have a seat," Passer says, friendly.

Close sits by her. Puts out his hand to her, says "Jimmy Close." She takes his hand, shakes it, smiles.

"I'm Catherine Jones. This is my boss, Kevin Kellogg."

Kellogg grunts, looks away from the hand Close offers.

"You're from West Virginia?" Kellogg asks.

"Yes," Close answers.

"Went to Princeton? Rutgers Law?"

"Yes."

"How you like it down here?"

"Washington? It's nice."

Kellogg looks out the window at the taxi that dropped Close off. The driver, a Middle Easterner, is filling out a log sheet.

"My father was a cabdriver," Kellogg says. "Here in D.C. I grew up here. Does that surprise you?"

"Why should it surprise me?" Close asks.

"A lot of people think D.C. is all black."

"It is mostly black."

"It is now. Wasn't always. In this city, when my father was a boy, if a black looked at a white the wrong way, the black could get beaten or killed. If you don't know Washington was a segregated Southern city, you don't know Washington."

Kellogg now looks Jimmy Close in the eye. "But now it's the other way around. You can take everything you think you know about race in America and throw it out, because you're through the looking glass here. This is a black city. You'll see, if you look for it, that whites don't make much eye contact with blacks on the street. That whites are the ones to move out of the way on the sidewalk if a black is walking toward them. You'll see, if you look for it, contempt in the eyes of the black city workers if your white ass ever asks anything of them. And if you get mugged, what are you going to tell the police—that a black male stuck a gun in your white face? That description, that crime, it isn't worth their time. Some of them might even be thinking that it's *good* you got mugged. Serves you right. Whitey."

Kellogg drags on his cigarette. Eyes Mr. Jimmy Close. "And knowing that, you want me to take, for a client, an organization which this city doesn't think has the right to exist? You know what people will say when they hear I'm working for you? They'll say, 'Figures.' Figures I'd work with a racist like you."

"The League of True Colors is not racist."

"What are you?"

"An anti-racist, pro-white special-interest group designed especially to protect poor whites, who are the most socially and politically ignored people in the country. An anti-defamation organization, which we need because whites as a race are constantly being defamed in the media."

"Why do you call it League of True Colors?" Passer asks.

"It's in opposition to the phrase People of Color, by which the media refer to nonwhites. That phrase says whites are people without color, which is a lie because we actually have more physical color diversity than any other race, and it's a racist degradation in the same way that referring to nonblacks as 'People of Intelligence' would imply that blacks were people with*out* intelligence."

Kellogg rolls his eyes in disgust. Asks, "What do you want from me?"

"The man who killed Henry James and his wife had nothing to do with us."

"So? The press accuses. You deny. The world goes on. What's your point? Richard Ells had nothing to do with you. So?"

"Henry James did."

"How?"

"I met with him just a week ago. We talked about a lot of things. Mostly LTC. And Henry James videotaped the meeting."

"Have you told the police about this?"

"I haven't spoken to them. My lawyer has. They didn't ask."

"They didn't ask about what connection you or LTC might have with Henry James?"

"They only asked about what connection we might have with Richard Ells. Their wording was poor on other, more general questions. If they ask directly if James and I met, I'll have to say yes, of course, if I say anything at all. But I'm not going to volunteer anything. You can understand how bad this would make me look. The press would get an awfully easy headline out of it. 'Henry James Murdered One Week After Meeting with LTC Head.' But I'm afraid word of the meeting might still come to light. I imagine the police, maybe the media, will investigate the victim's last days. Whether anyone will go back a week, I don't know."

"Other than the videotape, what evidence is there that this meeting took place?"

"I don't think there's any."

"How did it get scheduled? Your secretary calling his?"

"No. I was in town, lobbying on the Hill. I was upset about things. I made a spur-of-the-moment decision to call him. He invited me over. We talked late into the night."

"Where did you call from?"

"A pay phone. No check of his phone records will reveal anything."

"Do you take precautions against being tailed?"

"No."

"Maybe Ells tailed you."

Close thinks a moment. Says, "No. I called from the Rayburn Building. I don't think he could have gotten in there, or stayed near me without being conspicuous if he had. And I didn't leave by the same door I went in. I don't think he tailed me."

"But you can't be sure."

"No. And I can't be sure Martians didn't beam the information into his head."

"Exactly. Maybe this, maybe that. What are we left with?"

"The videotape."

"Why'd you make it?"

"We both thought it would be a good idea. We were in his living room, making small talk, and I saw the camera set up, and he told me they were going to tape his daughter's birthday the next day, and then his wife, Jessie, said, hey, this meeting might be kind of historic."

"Why historic?"

"I went over there because I'd been hearing so much about how the FBI might have penetrated us. One of our top speakers is retired FBI. And she's set up a faction within the organization that is much more extremist than I or my original followers are. I suspect maybe it's a deliberate FBI attempt to marginalize the movement. I went to Henry James because it's my sense of him that he's fair and intelligent, not at all anti-white, and I told him what I feared was happening. I was scared, and still am, with the whole movement now. I feel like it's getting away from me. This ex-FBI agent, Joan Price, she's more popular in my organization than I am. Anyway, I went to Henry James, and we talked. For hours. I don't know how else to put it: we just clicked. Right away. The most natural, immediate friendship I've ever had in my life."

"What did he have to say?"

"He said—and this is the unbelievable part—that I should disband the organization."

"What did you say?"

"At first I laughed. But we talked some more. And then I began to see his point."

"You agreed with him?"

"I was starting to."

"*That's* the unbelievable part."

"But he was right! In everything he said, he was right. That racial loyalty, no matter how well intentioned, is always, inherently, racist. That racial pride is always, inherently, foolish. He *talked* me into seeing the futility of it all. He talked me out of my own organization! But only because he didn't say anything I hadn't started to see myself already."

"What do you need the tape for?"

"I want the proof that it was a positive meeting. I'm scared that if word of the meeting somehow gets out, people might say we met and argued and I had him killed, or something equally simplistic. Unprovable, but media accusations don't need proof to be damaging. But I also want the tape for the reason we made it, which was to make a political statement that I was willing to be the first to lay down my gun, so to speak. Lay it down racially, I mean. Politically. Henry thought, and I agreed, that with my credibility among poor whites I could make a real statement, provide some real leadership away from the growing anger out there."

"You can still do that."

"And will. But the tape would help. This disbanding of LTC I have in mind, it has to be done right. I can't let it be seen as an act of cowardice. I certainly can't have people saying I'm afraid of an investigation into the James murders. We're being labeled racist fanatics by the press. We're being lumped in with the KKK. With militia groups. If I quit now, it'll look like I'm selling out my own people when they need me most. I need to prove that I was planning to break up LTC before Henry and Jessie got killed, not because of it. And I want it for Henry too. For his legacy. As proof to blacks that he was no Uncle Tom, he was the man who single-handedly talked me into disbanding what the NAACP call their number one enemy. If people, white and black both, can just hear him speak like he did that night, they'll be moved. They'll understand. They'll have to. I want that tape, Mr. Kellogg. I need it."

Kellogg sighs. "It's police property now, if it was at Henry's house or office. And if it wasn't there, then I can't guess where it would be."

"I at least need to know if they have it. And I can't just ask, because if they don't know about it, I don't want to tell them. I've heard that you still have good contacts in the department."

"That's it? You just want to know if they have this tape that for all I know might incriminate your sorry-assed self?"

Close breathes in and out a few times. Stays calm. "No. There's more."

"Tell me."

"I want to know why Ells used our initials as his blood signature."

"He was a psycho."

"I'm trusting my instincts here, but I just think it's too strange. We really didn't have anything to do with him, and we really aren't a white supremacist group."

"You're saying you've been framed?"

"Yes, I guess I am."

"And you want me to find out by who?"

"Yes."

"Let me tell you something. You didn't get framed. I'm going to take your case because if no one else will take it, I can get away with charging you double my usual rate. But I'm telling you up front, no one had two people killed to make you look bad. Making you look bad might be a fringe benefit, or a decoy, but it wasn't the reason. People just don't go that far."

"Which brings us to the other thing I want from you."

"Shoot."

"Maybe we weren't framed. Maybe Ells did work with people in LTC. I told you, there's a faction there now that is getting away from me. This ex-FBI agent, she's got a charisma I've never seen before. And she's building a following within the organization that scares me. I'm afraid that just maybe Ells *is* connected to LTC."

Kellogg takes that in. Says, "You want a lot."

"I do."

"Define it for me."

"I guess we'll say your job for this case is to find out what happened to the videotape of my meeting with Henry James; and to find out what, if anything, might connect LTC to Ells that I don't know about."

"All right. I want a ten-thousand-dollar retainer in my office tomorrow morning."

"Isn't ten thousand a lot?"

"What if it is?"

Close hesitates, then says, "Fine. Can I get daily reports?"

Kellogg nods.

Close stands. Puts out his hand for a shake. This time Kellogg takes it.

Close nods good-bye to Passer. Leaves.

Kellogg looks at Passer, who's looking down into her coffee cup.

"Oh, cut the shit," Kellogg says.

She looks up. At him. Sadly. "Me cut the shit?"

"Yeah."

"What shit is that?"

"The sensitive-liberal shit."

"I don't like the way you talk about black people."

"I don't like the way they talk about me. Last week, just

standing on a corner at Seventh and F, a carload of black girls drove by and yelled out 'Ofay motherfucker' at me. No reason. Just filled with hate and happy to show it."

With difficulty, because he's so fat and still a bit drunk, he slides out of the booth. Standing over her, he says, "We're going to make some easy money with this. Clear our debts. Buy ourselves some new equipment. Pad the hell out of our time sheets. You know, the usual fuck job on a sap client so we can take vacations this summer. And all I really have to do is make a few phone calls and then later, in my 'daily report,' talk a good game. Okay? Maybe we'll go to a few LTC meetings and look into this extremist faction he's talking about. But I'll find out if the police have the tape in one call. This is easy money. We need it."

She nods but doesn't look at him.

Kellogg listens to the music. Says of it, to Passer, "Ella Fitzgerald with Chick Webb."

"I don't care."

"You care about everything but not about anything. How you going to ever write that great book of yours if you don't care?"

"You're drunk."

Kellogg leans down close to her. She can smell the whiskey and coffee and cigarette and eggs on his breath. The stink of his underarms.

Kellogg whispers, "You're the luckiest person in the world. In baggy pants and shoulder pads and ball cap, you're a man. In anything else, you are definitely female. You can be black, Latino, or white. Whatever color's fashionable. Me? I'm a white man in a black city. I'm fat. I'm old. I'm ugly. I'm broke. I'm alone. My heart's got to go soon—there's a law of health that says so. You might be the person who cares about me most in this world, and you don't care about me much."

She faces him, eyes inches from his, water building in them. But the water's tension holds and the tears don't fall and she says only, "I want thirty bucks for every hour I bill on this case."

He steps back from her. Says, "Fine."

7

KELLOGG, IN HIS OFFICE, BELCHES. Moans. Drinks from his
pot of coffee. Moves his head about, trying to work out the
crick in his neck. Takes four aspirin, trying to soothe his
headache. Smokes. Calls out, "Sue, can you go downstairs
and get me an egg sandwich?"

"No," she calls back from her desk out front.

"Why not?"

"I'm doing my nails."

"Sue!"

"I'm serious!"

The phone rings.

"I suppose you want me to get that?" he asks.

"You are the most thoughtful man."

He answers. "Kellogg Investigations."

"Kevin? Hey."

"Hey, man." Kellogg recognizes the caller's voice. It's
the Black Detective. "Thanks for calling."

"What's up?"

"I'm on the case."

"Which case?"

"The monster."

"The James murders?"

"Yeah."

"How?"

"Jimmy Close."

"I heard he was looking for help. Also heard some wire that the Mayor's office was passing the word they'd be offended by anyone giving that help."

"I'm not on the Mayor's wire."

"No shit."

"So what's up?"

"This is some tender info I'm going to give you."

"I understand."

"Your line secure?"

"Checked it just yesterday. You at a pay phone?"

"Yeah. Okay. Listen, man. The Chief's holding a press conference this afternoon to announce the case is closed."

"Wow."

"Here's the scoop. This guy, Richard Ells, he videotaped himself doing it."

"That's all the rage among psychos."

"Yeah. And the tape showed he acted alone. Doesn't prove he wasn't put up to it by someone, but he was alone when he killed them, and it was definitely him that did the killing."

"How'd it go down?"

"At the point when he turns the camera on, he's got

them handcuffed. Then he ties them to their chairs. Henry— Did you know him? Personally?"

"A little."

"Henry's staying calm. So is Jessica. Henry's talking to Ells real calmly, saying he's got some money in his car and can get some more at the bank with his ATM card. Ells is just laughing, smiling, saying, 'Is that right? You got money? Got yourself this white woman here, like I ain't got? Got yourself a nice car, like I ain't got? Just high and mighty.' Anyway, Ells, he's just happy, tying them up and then gagging them. Good job of gagging too."

"Yeah? Bondage-type thing?"

"Kind of, but he didn't molest them, so I don't think he's that way. What he does next is, goes out of the picture, we presume into the kitchen, and comes back with a saw-toothed knife. Big old thing. And man, the only way to put it is, he just sets right in to sawing Jessica's head off."

The Black Detective goes quiet. Kellogg lets him have his silence.

"Anyway," the detective says, "Henry James, he sees this and starts going wild trying to get free, but he can't. Man. I mean, he had to watch his own wife get killed."

"Jesus."

After another moment's pause, the Black Detective says, "Ells, he was gone to the world. Had that soul-gone look in his eyes. You know? Vacant back there, like an addict?"

"I know the type."

"Henry James, that poor guy, he's going crazy against the ropes, but he can't get free, and after Ells gets done, he holds Jessica's head to Henry's face and says, 'Want a kiss good-bye?' And Henry, he's just finished. The fight is gone.

He's on the floor—he knocked himself over trying to get free—but now he's just staring into space. Ells grabs him by the hair and cuts his head off too."

"And you had to watch this shit."

"Aw, man, three fucking times I went over that tape. I tell you, brother, I surrender. I got twenty-seven years in. I'm done. I should have been gone long ago, but I am definitely out of here now. The Mayor's back. That's reason enough right there. You know how he feels about me."

"He don't forgive and forget."

It was the Mayor who'd demanded Kellogg's dismissal those many years before, when Kellogg and the Black Detective were both patrolmen, working together. When Kellogg had shot a black kid, who really *did* have a gun. The Black Detective, who'd been there, had testified that the gun was no plant; testimony that got Kellogg free of criminal charges; testimony given against the Mayor's "request" that he, the Black Detective, "remember" that it was dark in that alley and maybe he couldn't have really been sure the kid had a gun after all.

"And all the cutbacks coming in," the Black Detective says. "I hate deserting my town, but it's just gone to pieces."

"I know."

"Especially the force."

"I know."

"And this case, man, it's just the final straw. I didn't think this shit could still get to me, but it does. That mom and daughter killed in that drive-by last summer? I pulled that case. That two-year-old boy microwaved by his mother's boyfriend? I got that one. And now this. I mean, watching that sick motherfucker Ells do that. And that ain't the worst of it. Listen to this." He takes a deep breath. Heartbroken, says, "Okay. Ells, he takes Henry James's head and he uses it like a fucking paintbrush. Uses the neck part to paint the letters *LTC* on the wall. Then he real carefully puts the heads back on the corpses, which is hard to do because they're dead, their necks got no reason to help. He has to balance them. But then he hears a siren, like it's right outside the front door. It was a car on another call, but Ells, he hears it and panics. He bails out of the picture. On the video we can hear the back door open and bang shut. And then—and this is the fucker, man—then the little boy comes into the picture."

The detective can't speak for a moment. There's nothing Kellogg can say.

The detective lets out a long sigh. Says, tired, "The boy, he stands there, staring at it all. At his parents like that. How can he understand? I can't understand. How can a twelve-year-old?"

"Yeah."

"You know?"

"Yeah, man."

"This boy, he stares and stares, he's crying, he's shaking. Then we hear another squad car's siren. It was hard to tell which direction the sound came from, on the tape, but we checked the logs, and besides getting the exact time of death, we found out the first car had come down the street out front, and we think the second car was coming down the side street. There was a fight at a 7-Eleven a few blocks away, and a drunk hit an officer. Anyway, the boy, when he hears the siren, he snaps out of his shock or trance. And he does something weird. He goes to the television and grabs four videotapes from a stack there. And it must have been four exact tapes he wanted, because he pulled them out from under a pile of others. They were in movie boxes, and with some enhancement work we got the titles, but they don't mean anything that we can tell, and besides, why would a kid think to grab any tapes at all?"

"I don't know."

"You can't assume anyone, especially a child, is going to act logically in that situation, but still, that don't figure. He takes the tapes and runs out of the camera's picture in the direction of the back door, and just like when Ells left, we can hear the door open and shut."

"And that's the end of the tape?"

"Yeah."

"What else was on it?"

"Their daughter's birthday party. Ells started the tape just where the Jameses had left off, so it didn't have that much room left on it. After the boy left, the camera kept recording for a few minutes, until the tape ran out. But even that ain't the end of the shit. I saw the tape again just this morning? The Chief had had it, and some of the Mayor's fucks? Man, the part where the boy gets the videos and leaves, that's been erased."

"Why would they do that?"

"See? I don't know. But that's why I am done with this fucking department. Why would they do that? I don't know. I don't want to know."

"Yeah, you do."

"Yeah, I do. But I don't."

"How did they explain the erasure?"

"Accidental while switching from rewind to play."

"Yeah, okay."

"I'm done, man. I'm already gone. And I suggest you stay the fuck out of it too."

"You checked all Henry James's other tapes?"

"That was tedious, but yeah, we did. Nothing. I can't figure it. Best I can figure it is that, because the boy took children's movies, maybe they were comforting or something to him. Maybe he was emotionally attached to them. Maybe he's seen them with his parents a few times and he connects them to each other. Something."

"Did you get access to Henry's office?"

"Limited. Had ADAs hanging over me while I searched his files for anything related to Richard Ells or LTC. Nothing."

"Did he have any videotapes there?"

"I didn't think about that. But I'd remember seeing any, and I didn't."

"You check his den at home?"

"Yep."

"No tape of Henry James and Jimmy Close?"

"No. Why?"

Kellogg explains, then asks, "What's going on with the boy now?"

"We're stuck. You can read the papers for the straight scoop about what's happening with the boy. The area got grid-searched the morning the bodies were found. The boy's friends and classmates were interviewed. His grandmother. Rock Creek Park got dog-searched. Nothing."

"Figure it this way," Kellogg says. "The boy goes out to the alley. Ells is still there. Or near there, because it wouldn't take but a minute for him to figure out the siren he heard hadn't been for him. Ells sees the boy. Grabs him."

"That was my guess. Which don't leave us nowhere nice."

"You guys find Ells's car?"

"Nah. And there's none registered to him anywhere in the country."

"I'll still bet he had one. I don't figure a country white like him to be taking subways or buses around Washington, especially at night."

"Me, neither. And no cab company has a record of a drop-off on that block, not that their records mean shit."

"If Ells grabbed the boy and killed him there, the body would've turned up, so that's not it. If he'd taken the kid on foot, he would have had all night to bury the kid, but still, how's he going to be walking around D.C. with a kid that's screaming if he's alive, bleeding if he isn't, without getting any attention?"

"Don't seem likely."

"It's only a few blocks to Rock Creek Park, but they aren't dead blocks."

"If he got the kid, he had a car. Figure he takes the kid, dead or alive, out of town. But then he comes back? He'd have time, but it's still a tough guess."

"You guys check all unaccounted-for cars around there?"

"Yep."

"Go out to the suburban subway stops and check the parking lots there?"

"Yep. Had the dogs out sniffing the trunks. Nothing."

"Then what else figures? He grabbed the boy. Took him out of the city. Came back to the crime scene alone, just for the psycho fuck of it."

"How about: The boy's in shock. Wanders out into the woods. Curls up somewhere deep. Gets missed on the first go-through. Maybe meanders down to the Potomac and falls or jumps in. Maybe Ells took him to the Potomac. And then again, there's the tabloid theory. Theories."

"I've heard them."

"That Ells wasn't acting alone. That LTC did this and they've got the boy."

"And they left their initials painted in blood on the walls. Right."

"I said it was tabloid."

"Is there anything connecting Ells to LTC, besides that he went to a meeting?"

"No. The FBI's position is that it might be a kidnap, so they're following that up. But they got nothing to work with, far as I know. And the agents assigned to it, they are the worst. The same sorry-ass morons who've been assigned to investigate corruption in the Mayor's new administration. I spoke to some other agents. They said these four agents are known within the division as the Goof Squad, because they're such idiots. Like the Director pulled the four worst agents he could find in the whole FBI into one squad."

"Speaking of idiots, is there anything more to Mallory's involvement than meets the eye?"

"You can call John Mallory a lot of things, but idiot isn't one of them."

"I know."

"And no, it seems to have been a straight thing. There

was talk about him being a Jack Ruby here. Believe it or not, there's been some demand for an investigation into whether John's connected with LTC or Ells. But the Mayor's fucks squashed that idea."

"John's always been tight with them."

"His dick must have got hard when the Mayor got reelected. But as to him shooting Ells, he was home when the call went out for all day-shift detectives to come in early and help out on this, and he didn't get there ahead of no one. It isn't like he could have planned on being called in, or being assigned to that particular street and all."

Kellogg and the Black Detective talk for another hour, going over the same ground again.

After hanging up, the Black Detective thinks about how long he's been doing this. About how he and Kellogg and Mallory were in the same cadet class back in '68. Had only two weeks under their belts when the riots came.

Fought together. He and Mallory hadn't been close the way he and Kellogg had, but Mallory had been a true liberal on a force that was still real white then. And Mallory had joined him in supporting the Mayor's first candidacy. But Mallory had become friends with the Mayor and stuck with the Mayor long after it became obvious to the Black Detective that the Mayor was corrupt and the police force being destroyed, so he and Mallory were no longer friendly. But he and Kellogg, that was different. He remembered especially Kellogg's willingness to stand up to the white racist sergeants who ran things back then, and he couldn't remember many other whites who had.

8

ON TELEVISION A MAN IS SAYING, in a steady, solemn voice, "When whites wrote of a Garden of Eden they meant Africa, where all humans lived in peace, harmonious with nature. But there was among us there a sick brother, a physical and spiritual weakling, who ate of the tree of knowledge, and by this is meant began developing technology. Our African ancestors caught this wicked brother in his blasphemous act and drove the defiler out of Eden. He ran north to the ice country, where he lost his color and became as to ice as we are to earth, the same in color, the same in spirit. There in the frozen north, living like an animal in caves, the defiler mad scientist spawned a race of devils and developed the technology by which he, thousands of years later, angry about his physical inferiority, angry about his expulsion from Eden, came back and enslaved us."

The speaker is a young black man. A light-skinned, quick-featured young man with a great smile who isn't smiling. He's staring sternly into the camera. He's wearing a black suit, white shirt, bright green-red-and-brown striped tie. That's the New Africa uniform. This is the *New Africa* show, broadcast weekly on the Black Television Network cable channel. With him, behind him, is a line of other young people, dressed the same way, expressing the same way. Their leader, this speaker, is Khalid. One name. Khalid.

"I say, my people, what I always say, and what you know to be true, every one of you—we will never be free in the white man's country. It is only with the creation of our *own* country that we can be our own people. Only with the creation of New Africa, a land of freedom from white oppression.

"And do not doubt that we can do this. For we have a weapon before which the white is powerless—his hatred of us. Yes, you heard me right. We can use the white man's hatred for us against him. I say, my beautiful people, do to the whites what they fear most. Fulfill their own worst stereotypes of us."

Khalid's long and slender fingers are intertwined before him, prayer-like. His head is tilted forward so that he is peering intensely out from under his eyebrows.

"Understand the devil," he says. "Understand his breeding.

"First among the devil's kind is the Jew, killer of the black man Jesus, the most cunning of our enemies, who manipulates the world by controlling the movies, the television, the newspapers. And we can never forget that the holocaust he suffered is but a drop in the bucket compared to the holocaust he perpetrated on us by masterminding the slave trade, is but a drop in the bucket compared to the genocide we are suffering even now.

"Next most evil is the Asian, by far the most inferior, a weakling who branched off from the sick brother we banished to Europe and who bred like vermin to number in the billions. The Asian is here now, infiltrating our neighborhoods with the help of Jew bankers, to take our money, our hope.

"Next most evil is the common white, a pathetic tool of the Jew, always the overseer, never the overlord. His role in the devil's world is to police us, which the Jew and Asian are afraid to do themselves. White men prostitute themselves as abusers of law in the name of law; his women prostitute themselves because it is the devil's way to tempt us with the whore-slut.

"And last among the devil's people is the Latino, lackey to his white masters, brought here to do the work we refuse to do ourselves. Creatures of so little pride they will gladly be maids or dishwashers, ditchdiggers and busboys; like the Asian, short, and spiteful for it."

Khalid isn't always so radical, but he knows that this is just another cable show to most people watching, which means he might have only a few seconds to get people's attention before they use their remote control.

Joan Price is among those watching. She's a middle-aged white woman, short, stocky, with badly permed, tightly curled brown hair. She watches Khalid. She records the show. She takes notes.

When it ends she turns off the television and leans back on her couch, tired. Always tired, never quitting.

She looks up at the wall. At a picture of her husband and daughter.

Six months ago they were here, in their suburban Maryland house. Joan was not here. She was working. FBI Special Agent Joan Price. Outstanding Joan Price. Working.

She came home that night. She called out for them when she came in the front door, and when they didn't answer she went downstairs, expecting to find them playing Ping-Pong or doing homework. Instead she found her nightmare.

Her husband's body was stuffed in a closet, as if the killer thought hiding it would help. Joan Price had found that body first and, trembling but thinking, searched the house, gun drawn, not knowing if she wanted to find her daughter. But she did find her. In her room upstairs. Thirteen years old. Beaten to death with her own baseball bat.

Joan stared at that body. She didn't faint or scream or cry. She stared. And felt a monster rise in herself. The devil. Because on a part of the bloody sheet that still was white, the sheet on which her blond daughter lay with brains spilled and face destroyed, was a hair. A kinky black hair. Which Joan decided belonged to a black man. And on the floor, poking out from under the bed, was an empty forty-ounce beer bottle. About which she reached the same conclusion.

Joan Price has grown up here in Prince George's County. She sees the hair, the forty, knows how black is crime in this county, doesn't call 911. Gets an unregistered handgun she's had for years. Gets in her car. Drives. Deep into the city. Slowly down a block. The right block. The wrong one. First and Kennedy Northwest.

A black man sees her. Waves her down. Assumes she's after what white women driving around here at this time of night are usually after.

Hey baby, what you looking for? I got what you need.

Joan looks around. Sees no one else. Asks the man for what she knows he's got.

He says, Yeah, you know I got that.

She says, Good, boy, that's good.

His eyes widen at the "boy," but it ain't no thing, just business.

She reaches in her handbag.

He thinks it's for money.

Quick is that gun in his face.

She stares at him. Devil in her. Hate.

One, two, three, four seconds go by. She stares at him, not breathing, not shaking, not scared.

He starts to say something. Doesn't get to.

When his body is found the next day, it seems to be just another clueless drug kill.

She goes home and calls 911 to report finding her family murdered. And as she waits, in the bloody house, with that unregistered gun in her hand, for the police to arrive, she holds that gun to her own head. What if she's wrong about who killed her family? She's panicking, thinking of that. What if she's wrong? She knows it isn't only blacks who might have kinky black hair, it isn't only blacks who buy forty-ounce beers, and it isn't only blacks who commit murder. She decides to kill herself if she's wrong.

Her family's killer was quickly identified. A black man. He'd been visiting cousins down the street, and when those cousins, nervous about him anyway because they knew his history, heard about the murders, they called the police, intuiting that their visitor might have had something to do with it. He was easily found, instantly confessed. He'd done it before, been caught before, confessed before, been sentenced before. He said he needed money. Targeted the Price house. Climbed in through a second-floor window after seeing that Mr. Price and his daughter went down to the basement. He said he hadn't wanted to kill anyone, but when the girl had come back upstairs and caught him, he'd had to silence her. He'd beaten her instead of shooting her to keep the noise down, but when he'd then heard her father calling up for her, he'd forced him at gunpoint back down the stairs and shot him.

At the killer's sentencing hearing, Joan was allowed to address the court. She ignored the court.

She spoke to the killer. Screamed at him. Held nothing back.

Her testimony, taped, was played first on local television, then nationally. It was captivating. The black man sitting passively, stone-faced; the white mother and wife, devastated, ferocious.

Joan received letters afterward, even donations. Sympathy.

She had a personal meeting with the director of the FBI. He asked what he could do for her. She told him she wanted a special assignment.

"Name it," he said.

"LTC," she said.

"The white organization?"

"Right."

"That's interesting. We've already been working on a plan to investigate it. We're in every other white supremacist group. LTC hasn't actually been proven to be racist, but we're under pressure to show that it is."

"Let me do it."

"Why you?"

"I've heard from them. Been invited to speak to them."

The Director smiled. Said, "Great. That's perfect. You'll have to publicly resign from the FBI first, because you've been identified as an agent by the media. A false resignation, of course, and just for the duration of the assignment."

"When can I start?"

"Right away?"

"Okay."

"Let's have you report directly to me."

"Okay."

"Take your time on this. Work your way in slowly. Give that speech. Do some homework first, so you'll have a better idea of what they want to hear. Earn their trust. Work your way up their ladder."

Joan did that. Earned LTC's trust. Worked her way up the organizational ladder. Only she didn't do it slowly. She was too good. Her enthusiasm was too sincere, her talent too obvious. She kept media attention because she proved such a good guest on talk shows, with her articulate expressions, her victim's résumé, her compelling presence. Someone called her a white Malcolm X. The tag stuck. Joan Price. Joan d'Arc Price. FBI special agent supposedly on an undercover mission to find and expose criminal conduct at LTC.

But Joan Price was a step ahead of the Director on that. Because there was no way she was going to hurt LTC. She wouldn't gather evidence against them, because it was her role as an undercover agent that was false. Her work for LTC was her true mission. She would not again settle merely for killing a drug dealer, because the killing of whites was a minor part of the race war she thought blacks were waging. Politics was the bigger part. So it was through politics that she'd give them the war she thought they wanted. She'd give them a war they wouldn't believe. Joan Price. White Malcolm.

She records the *New Africa* show. Stays on the channel as a rap video program comes on. Notes the portrayal, in one video, of Jesus as a black man, Satan as a white. Notes, in another video, critics of rap portrayed as incredibly ugly, obese whites. In several others, white cops as oppressors, black suspects as innocent.

She reads *Emerge, Ebony, Jet* magazines and clips examples of what she sees as their black-is-better egotism.

Reads the black local columnists in the *Washington Post* with what she sees as their white-hating diatribes.

Reads black-authored novels in which whites are evil cartoon-like characters, hatred of whom is justified.

Watches movies made by black directors, which she sees as excusing of anti-white violence, supportive of white-blaming conspiracy theories, contemptuous of white culture, mocking of white fears.

Joan Price pulls it all together into an incredibly effective presentation, which she can give without referring to notes, she has it down so pat. A presentation effective in "proving" that blacks hate whites. That the war is on. That "we" have to fight back. That "they" hate "us."

9

KEVIN KELLOGG IS SPLAYED BACK on the tattered green couch in his office, settled into the cushions crushed under his huge butt. He's watching the Chief's news conference, held at the BTN studio, at which the Mayor has also showed, happy to get the spotlight of what he expects to be a positive moment.

The Chief states the case, which is that the tape Ells made of the murders proves he acted alone, at least for the actual killing. Whether he had conspiratorial aid has not been convincingly determined, but as yet no evidence has turned up. The FBI will be handling the continuing investigation into Ells's possible white supremacist connections. As to the boy, all efforts have been made to find him, but as yet nothing has turned up. The tape Ells made—which will *not* be released for public viewing, out of consideration for the victim's family—does show the boy at the crime scene, just after Ells stepped out of the picture. But then the tape ends.

Our best supposition, the Chief says, is that Ells grabbed the boy, and (his voice changes, from distantly professional to personal) because we have not been able to locate the child and have searched everywhere, with the community's help, for which we are grateful, we have to assume that Ells killed the boy. Ells killed the Jameses before midnight and was himself killed the next morning. That would leave plenty of time for him to take the boy away, dispose of the body somewhere, and come back. Our prayers are with this missing child, and we *will* maintain due vigilance in our continued search for him. But we have no leads.

Reporter: What about the LTC connection? Any more word on that?

Chief: As I stated, the FBI is handling that investigation. They have looked into the possibility of a kidnapping, and their treating the case as a possible kidnapping will give them specific jurisdiction. But again, I don't want to give false hope.

The Mayor steps up, puts his hand on the Chief. Both are upper-middle-aged black men, gray-haired, pudgy. They have little else in common.

The Mayor: My brothers and sisters, let us begin the healing process with a minute of silence.

His all-black, mostly female staff bend their heads on cue. About thirty seconds pass.

The Mayor: This has been a great tragedy for our city, and yet it is not a surprising tragedy. Words have meaning, and the vile hate talk of Republican politicians and white male radio hosts is ultimately responsible for this murder. Henry James was not a perfect man, but he was a black man, and even though he was seduced away from us, he was still one of us, as is the boy, his child, lost to us but found in God's great hands. The blame here is not with Henry James but with the hatemongers, the bigots, who want to go back to a time of hate, who want to take back our affirmative action, who impose upon our city the overseer council of Uncle Toms who, as we suffer here today, can only think about how to fire more of us from our jobs. These are terrible, frightening times for African America, but Henry James and his child are not to blame. Maybe we won't ever be able to prove that LTC is behind the killings. They are a slick outfit and surely thought this assassination out in advance. But we know in our hearts how evil they are, and even if the proof is not found, or is found but not made public, we *know* words have meaning, and those who push for hate are to blame.

Reporter: Mr. Mayor, are you saying the Republicans are to blame for this?

The Mayor: Black people didn't kill Henry James.

Reporter Two: Mr. Mayor, are you taking questions about the New Africa Security Contract?

The Mayor, scowling: That is not the issue here. Why do you bring that up? That is a perfectly legal contract to a righteous organization.

Reporter Three: Mr. Mayor, what about the Chinatown land-deal kickback? New allegations—

The Mayor, interrupting, indignant: That land deal was perfectly legal, and the people of this city know it.

Reporter Four: Any comment about the work done on your house—

The Mayor, interrupting again, angry: Why is it that anytime a black man tries to get ahead in this country you whites have to drag him down? Why are you so afraid of a

black man's success? I will not be a party to the further
persecution of African America by the racist media.

He storms off the stage, followed by his staff.

Michael Ottaway comes on. Announces that the press
conference is over, thank you all for coming. The station cuts
to a commercial.

Kellogg, seeing Ottaway, thinks about that. He was told that
Ottaway would be promptly dismissed, yet here the man is,
still working. It might not mean anything more than that
BTN just hasn't found the right moment to fire him, or
maybe Ottaway is involved in a project that they need to have
him finish, or maybe he just talked himself out of trouble. But
Kellogg thinks about it anyway. About being paid cash.
Hasn't stopped thinking about that. Kellogg, jaded, cynical,
from all the ugliness he's witnessed as a cop and as a private
investigator, sees life in terms of schemes, manipulations, lies,
and cover-ups. Prides himself on seeing those things. On
seeing the truth behind the requests the world makes of him.
He doesn't mind being a party to other people's schemes. He
just minds not knowing what the real scheme is. And by
instinct, he's never been satisfied with what BTN was up to
when they hired him to document Ottaway's sexual harassment and then paid him cash. He isn't even sure it's fair to say
that BTN hired him at all, because he dealt with only one
person there, a woman in the Human Resources office. He
checked that she did indeed work there. But he was always
surprised that the owner was not involved in this himself. The
woman said that the owner wasn't comfortable investigating
Ottaway because they were old friends.

Kellogg drinks from his coffeepot. Rubs out one

cigarette, lights another. Thinks. Calls Ottaway, who isn't back to his office. Leaves a message on his voice mail.

Kellogg, with Sue Cline, goes downstairs to the coffee shop, bringing his cellular phone. But except for Passer calling to say she's up (it's noon) and ask if she's working today (she is), there are no calls.

Back in his office, Kellogg again calls Ottaway. This time he leaves a message that he's calling about "Sheila," which was Passer's undercover name in the case.

The phone rings a minute later. Kellogg answers. "Kellogg Investigations."

Silence.

"Mr. Michael Ottaway, how are you? This is Kevin Kellogg. Recognize my name?"

"You're the motherfucker who framed me with that bitch Sheila."

"Her name's not Sheila."

"I know that now."

"And she's not a bitch."

"Who gives a shit?"

"Fine. Mr. Ottaway, we need to talk."

"Why?"

Kellogg laughs. "Because I'm the motherfucker who framed you."

"So what do you want?"

"What do you care? Just come over. And on the way, think about what *you* want."

"Tell me what you want."

"No, Mr. Ottaway. Your phone's tapped." Kellogg doesn't actually know that, but it might be true.

Ottaway goes quiet.

Kellogg gives him his address. Says to be there in one hour. Hangs up. Calls Passer, who's still home, waking up. Tells her to come in now, because he needs her to do something before Ottaway arrives. She's there twenty minutes later, in sweat clothes and sneakers.

Kellogg gives her one of the glossies of her with Ottaway. Tells her to write a note on it and sign it. Tells her what to write. Tells her he'll explain later, wait downstairs.

Ottaway enters the front room. Doesn't speak.

Sue Cline says, "Hello, Mr. Ottaway, you can just go on in. Mr. Kellogg is waiting for you." She points to the door.

Ottaway enters Kellogg's office. Looks around the room as if it's diseased. He's dressed in a very expensively tailored suit. He's tall, handsome, affectedly austere.

"Shut the door," Kellogg says.

Ottaway, after an arrogant hesitation, shuts it. Looks at Kellogg, who can't help smiling.

"Mr. Ottaway. Sir. How are you?"

Ottaway glares. Kellogg laughs. Says, "Man, don't try that powerful-executive shit with me. I don't care how much money you make. I know who you really are."

Ottaway looks sheepish.

"Let's cut to the chase, Ottaway. What do you want?"

"What do *I* want? *You're* the one who called this meeting."

Kellogg can't help laughing again. He's too amused. "What do you want?" he asks again.

"*You* called the meeting!" Ottaway repeats. "What do *you* want?"

"I know what I want. And in fact, I know what you want. But, Mr. Ottaway, I'd like you to *tell* me what you want."

Ottaway shakes his head.

"You can sit if you want," Kellogg says.

"Fuck you."

Kellogg laughs again. Says, "You the one who produces that Saturday-night comedy hour?"

Ottaway nods reluctantly.

"Man, that's a funny show," Kellogg says. "I never knew black people could be so funny. Man, I just laugh and laugh and laugh at them. There was that one guy, all he did was come out onstage, look around, and say, 'Kill Whitey,' and everybody laughed so loud. Me, too."

A moment passes.

With a bit of a pout, Ottaway says, "You can't give me what I want."

"Yes I can," Kellogg says. He now looks, speaks, steadily, confidently, right at Ottaway.

"You can undo this shit?" Ottaway asks.

"Sure."

"How?"

"You haven't told me . . ."

"I want out of trouble on the sexual harassment thing!"

"Who set you up on that?"

"You. And that bitch who works for you."

"That's right."

Another moment passes. When Kellogg sees a look of conciliation come to Ottaway's face, he says, "Sit down."

Ottaway does.

"Here's your story. You were working *with* us, Mr. Ottaway. We were doing an instructional video about sexual harassment and went to you for your professional assistance. You agreed to help us because it's such an important issue to you. You used to be the kind of man who took advantage of women who worked under him, and as an act of contrition, and as a sign of your own raised consciousness, you volunteered your time. The photos I took of you and my operative at the bar that one night, that was just role playing."

Ottaway is thinking. He nods very slightly.

Kellogg pushes a piece of paper across the desk. "This is a letter from Kellogg Investigations thanking you for working with us on this very important issue."

Ottaway picks it up. Reads it.

Kellogg next pushes an eight-by-ten photograph over.

Ottaway picks it up. It's a picture of him and Passer having dinner. On the photo Passer has written, "Michael, thank you so much for your help. You know, you talked so much about your wife and daughters that I feel like I know them! They are certainly lucky to have such an enlightened man in their lives!"

She'd signed it, "Gratefully, Catherine 'Sheila' Jones."

Kellogg lets it sink in.

Ottaway says, resigned, voice low, "So what do *you* want?"

"I want to know why."

"Why they wanted the shit on me?"

"Yeah."

Ottaway looks down. Says, to the floor, "No you don't."

"Try me. Starting with who 'they' are."

Looking back up, Ottaway smiles and says, "Why?"

"I don't like being used. And I get the feeling I was. I get the feeling this isn't about sexual harassment."

"No."

"Which means the woman over there just wanted something on you. Wanted a thumb on you. Used me to get it."

"Yes."

"A thumb not just on your job but on your life. On your marriage, which is pretty good in spite of you. On your career, which would be over if there was undeniable proof that you're a sexist asshole."

"I'm not an asshole. I don't treat women that way. It was just Sheila. Or whatever her name is. I never met anyone so . . . you know."

"She's a pretty woman."

"No, I deal with pretty women all the time. She's more than that."

"And all you could think to do was use your power to fuck her?"

"It's all she responded to!"

Kellogg waves his hands. "Back to the thumb on you. Who wants it?"

Ottaway takes a deep breath. The look of a man with a bursting secret comes over his face. Kellogg knows the look well. He saw it a lot as a cop. The look of a confessor.

"I don't know if you can handle it," Ottaway says snidely. "You probably won't believe it."

Kellogg is silent. Ottaway goes on.

"You know what New Africa is?"

Kellogg nods.

"They're in the other half of the building with us. BTN's owner doesn't have anything personally to do with them, doesn't even like them. But some of the staff mem-

bers do. The woman who hired you is a New African.
Anyway, she'd approached me about helping New Africa
because I'd said before that I liked Khalid's message. She
said they wanted to do a video surveillance, for security, but
they didn't know anything about the equipment. She asked
me to help. I said get me when you need me. And then one
day these three New Africans tell me they'll need my help
with this thing. I went along. Like all my talk about doing
my part for the cause, like that talk had a momentum of its
own. Okay, so they pull up their car and we load it with the
video equipment and go to this motel out on New York
Avenue. We set up a hidden camera in one room and
monitor it from the next room. I'm nervous with these
three guys, because, I don't know, they were scary. One of
them asked me if I'd ever been in prison, and when I said
no, they all laughed. I wasn't liking any of it, but I had to
see it through, you know?

"So maybe two hours later, we're in action on the next
room. A white man comes in with a hooker, a black hooker,
only she's a he, you know. I'm calling her a her, but it's a
him. Okay, they enter the room, and me and the New
Africa guys, we're watching the monitor, and the white
man, he looks familiar to me, but I can't place him at first,
and then they tell me it's the director of the FBI. That
freaks me, because I've been smelling some deep shit, and
now I know what it is. These motherfuckers are getting shit
on the man. I want out, but what can I do? Right? Okay, so
this sick shit goes down. I mean, this hooker, she's tying this
man up, and whipping him, and fucking his ass. Man, I
didn't watch, really. But I heard the New Africans giggling
and one of them talking about how he knew the bitch from

prison. Okay, so it ends in the next room. And the hooker, she tells the Director she wants more money. He tells her to fuck herself. A couple of minutes ago *he* was *her* bitch, but now he's a man again, right? And he throws a twenty on the floor and tells her not to forget that one word from him and she's right back in prison. He leaves. The New Africans, they take the tape we made, turn off the monitor, and tell me to wait there a minute. They go out, and a second later I hear talk in the next room. I can't help it, I turn the monitor back on."

He lets out a deep sigh. Scrunches his eyes tightly closed. His hands go to his face, rub his temples. He says softly, hurt, "They killed her. The hooker. Him. They beat him to death with their fists. Took a table lamp and crushed his skull."

Ottaway looks up at Kellogg. "You understand?"

Kellogg nods.

Ottaway says, "They got the Director on tape, in that room with that whore, the same day her body will be found by the police. Who's not going to know he's the one who killed her? They even had her mention that she was going to the Bullets-Lakers game that night. You know how often the Lakers come to town?"

"Once a year."

"So it dates the videotape. They even had her mention some new player the Lakers had, so not even the year would be in question."

"Then what?"

"Then the New Africans came back. I'd turned the monitor off, because I sure didn't want them to know I'd seen what they'd done. They'd washed up in the bathroom, but there was still blood on their clothes. They asked me if I'd heard anything. I said no. Some yelling, maybe. They said they'd had to hit the hooker a few times to keep her in line. They said I could wait in the car while they got the equipment together. Thanks for showing them how to set it all up. I went out to the car. They drove me back to BTN.

"That night, the New African woman at BTN calls me. Asks me how it went that day. I said fine. She asked me what happened. I told her we got the director of the FBI on a blackmail tape. She said cool. Asked me what about the hooker. I said I didn't know anything about her. She asked me if I wanted to do more work with New Africa. I said not really, no. She asked why. I said I just didn't feel comfortable with them. Then she was quiet. I started talking, like an idiot, saying I liked them all right and believed in what they were about; I just didn't feel comfortable doing things like that. She didn't say anything. Just let a minute pass and then hung up. I never heard anything more about it. Never saw anything in the paper about any hooker's body being found, either."

"A hooker murder ain't exactly pressworthy these days."

"No."

"So. The New African woman who got you involved gets nervous. She'd probably vouched for you with Khalid, and then when you got shy, she, or they, got nervous. Not drastically nervous, or they'd have killed you. Just a little nervous. Wanted a little insurance. Called me. Set it up in a manner in keeping with this woman's position at BTN."

Ottaway nods.

"Take the glossy," Kellogg says. "And the letter. They'll

clear you with your wife anyway, if the subject ever comes up. And I will back you on the story, that the sexual harassment was just role playing. But do yourself a favor—get a job someplace else."

Ottaway nods. He knows.

10

SOLEMN LONG RAY MOVES DOWN AN ALLEY, comfortable there, in the dark. He's wearing blue jeans, boots, and a hooded sweatshirt, the hood pulled over his brow.

He's spent this day letting the city know he is back. Tracking down people he knows. Asking questions as coolly as possible. "What's up with that murder? That Henry James murder? What you think about that boy being gone?" Asking like his is just the same curiosity everyone has, nothing more.

But he's only got rumors (those LTC people got the boy and tortured him/sold him/killed him; the police did it, 'cause Henry James was investigating them). He hasn't heard any stories he couldn't have invented himself. And his attempt to find Chavez has been pointless. He went to an old address his mother had for the man, but no one there knew him, or would admit it to a six-ten black man.

He called the Mayor's office. Left a message. Called back. Left another message. Called a third and fourth time.

Now he walks across the city, at night, looking in the windows of nice restaurants where well-dressed white people are eating; past emptying office buildings of the sort he's never been in for any good reason; through the blacker and blacker, tougher and tougher residential neighborhoods of Northwest Washington, until he's deep into Northeast Washington, on a commercial block off New York Avenue. Single- and double-story broad warehouse buildings, fast food, cheap motels. Skyscrapers aren't allowed in Washington, so its buildings flow gently over its slight rises. It's a beautiful, tree-filled city for the most part. Not this part.

He comes to a new, red-brick, two-story building. The sign there says: NEW AFRICA. He peers through the dark glass windows, into the well-lit lobby. Sees four men in black suits, white shirts, brightly striped ties. The New Africa uniform.

Long enters the lobby and the four men stand, move to confront him.

"Can I help you, brother?" asks one, looking up at Long, as they all must.

"I'm here to see Khalid."

"Do you have an appointment?"

"No."

"You have to have an appointment."

"No I don't."

The other three men stand behind the speaker, ready to back him up but not liking the prospect. The speaker takes a more aggressive posture and vocal tone. "If you don't have an appointment, you have to leave, brother."

Long smiles slightly. Death-looks the four men, none of whom can hold his gaze. He comes from a place, has seen things, in himself and others, that set him apart and above other men in any situation of threat or fear. He's hard at a higher level.

"Pick up the phone," he commands. "Call Khalid. Tell him I'm here. He'll see me."

As an act of appeasement, looking put out, the man speaking for the four says, "What's your name?" as he picks up the phone on the desk.

"You just tell him what I look like. If he wants you to know my name, he'll give it to you."

The man pushes a button on the phone. After a moment, he speaks into it, saying only, "It's some really tall guy who says he knows Khalid." After a moment, he says, "Yeah, I guess so." After another moment, he hangs up. Looks up at Long with respect and relief. He lets his breath out. Says, to the others, "It's okay."

The others also look relieved. Long shakes his head, disgusted.

Though it's only a two-story building, it has an elevator. That elevator opens, and the handsome, light-skinned Khalid steps out, followed by two pretty, long-legged, big-bottomed young women in the female version of the New Africa uniform—black skirt and pumps, white blouse, bright green and brown and red scarf.

Khalid beams as he grabs Long, who smiles genuinely back at him.

"Remember this man," Khalid says to the others. "Remember his face. He is the man referred to in my book as the Tall One. The man who gave me hope and help during my year in the Slave Pens."

Khalid leads Long, with the two silent women, into the

elevator, then upstairs, into his well-furnished office suite. Another young woman and two other men, all in uniform, are in the anteroom, at a desk. Khalid introduces Long to them.

"Our fine New African women, they do not suffer the white disease of gender fear, gender hate. Because of our basic precept of respect for women, they are comfortable in their respect for men. Satisfied with their role as leaders, not of nations, but of families. This is the natural way, the African way, which has been corrupted by weakling white males, whose women revolt from sexual and moral dissatisfaction. But our women seek only to bring happiness to the world."

By this speech, Long understands that Khalid is telling him the women are available.

Long says, "Let's talk."

Khalid smiles. "Of course. You want a drink? Soft drink, of course."

Long shakes his head no. He and Khalid go alone into Khalid's large private office and shut the door behind them. Khalid sits grandly behind his broad oak desk with its computer and phone. Long looks at the expensive furniture. Without sitting, he says, "You're doing well."

"*We* are doing well. You know I haven't forgotten you. You got the money I sent?"

Long nods. Khalid had sent a man to meet him when he was released from prison. That man had given him three thousand dollars.

"That's one of our promises to the people," Khalid says. "Three thousand dollars, a car, and first month's rent and deposit on an apartment to all freed slaves. For you, of course, there's a lot more than that." He hesitates only a moment, then asks, "You wanted some private time, you said, before coming to see me, since getting out? Why? I mean, it's okay, of course."

"I didn't want to rush back into the world. I wanted to just be slower about the adjustment than I was last time. I didn't want to fuck right back up again."

"But I could have helped you with that."

"Don't take it personally, man."

"I know, I know."

"And thanks for arranging for me to get out of that halfway house bullshit."

"That was easy. A call from me to the Mayor, from the Mayor to whoever runs that office. Done."

"The Mayor," Long says derisively. "I been calling the motherfucker, but he won't talk to me. What's up with him?"

"Don't worry, we got him."

"You sure?"

"Absolutely. Long, we got him all boxed up. Thanks to the work you did with him while he was inside."

Long smiles, and Khalid does too.

"Motherfucker can get busted for crack and get re-elected anyway," Long says. "But one look at him getting a blow job from a white woman, and his ass is cooked."

While in prison, the Mayor received visits from prostitutes, one of whom was white. Long had made these arrangements and also arranged for one such meeting to be videotaped.

"He's not a true believer, of course," Khalid says. "He doesn't care about anyone or anything except himself. If he was white he'd be George Wallace. But that's okay. In his own way, he's very predictable. We probably don't even need that tape. Still, you know how I believe in insurance."

"Uh-huh."

"Anyway, man, brother, we got it so going on, it's scary. We got multimillion-dollar contracts with the city for housing-project security, for Afrocentric education, for commercial development. We've got a theater, two restaurants, a music and book store. We've got branches in New York, L.A., Detroit, and of course the big one, Atlanta. We got the Mayor in our pocket because of that prison tape, we got the FBI director because of that frame-up murder we did, and we got the Chief locked up with the riot tape."

"That's all right."

"And with our pull on the Director, we had him set up what we call a Goof Squad. Check this out. The Director, he pulls together the four most incompetent, idiotic, and racist agents in the force. White guys so fucking worthless no one wants to work with them anyway. He assigns this Goof Squad to investigate political corruption in D.C. They are so stupid, these guys, they can't find shit. But even if they did, we all got an out, because these Goof Squad fucks are all documented racists, so their testimony wouldn't mean shit even if they did find something. Understand?"

"That's slick."

"It is. I'm telling you, brother, it's all going to happen. We got to take our time and do it right, but it will happen. I've got the psychology down, just like we used to talk about all them long old nights in the joint. The psychology of the black man to pull him together. The psychology of the white to rip him apart. And the Simpson verdict. What a blessing that was. God is great."

"I hear that."

"Now tell me, what do you want to do now?"

"I don't know."

Khalid nods. "No need to rush into anything. Whatever you want you got. In the meantime, go see Personnel tomorrow. Get on the payroll. Fifteen hundred a week."

Long smiles. Nods his head. Khalid, seeing Long smile, is happy.

"That money, that's yours if you want to do anything or not, you understand. That's just yours. The people owe you for what you've done for me. You can just come in once a week and pick up your check, no problem."

"I might do that for a while."

"No problem."

"I got some personal things to take care of."

"Don't get yourself in trouble."

"I won't."

"If you got scores to settle, let me know. We've got men on staff, women too, who can do what needs to be done."

"I'm all right."

They look at each other. Khalid gets up, goes to Long, hugs him again. Says, "I am so glad to see you. I need you, brother."

He and Long talked a great deal about political philosophy while in prison. Especially Long's views, which Khalid had eaten up, about the nature of political emotions with respect to issue positioning, preemptive accusation, and aggressive claims of victimization. Long, the English teacher's son, thought of writing a book about what he'd learned of human nature, of politics, in prison, a world of cut-throat deceptiveness and fatal clique errors. A Machiavelli-type book. But instead of writing it he told it, over and over, to Khalid, refining it in response to Khalid's probing questions until he tired of it himself but with interest and pride later watched Khalid apply it through New Africa.

Khalid gets a look on his face. Long, knowing him well, asks what's wrong.

Khalid says, "Brother, there's one big thing fucked up right now."

"Go ahead."

"I hate to hit you with this, you just out, but I got no one else I can really go to."

"What?"

Khalid, sighing, says, "The tapes are missing."

Long shakes his head, sad.

"I know, man," Khalid says. "We got some treasonous motherfucker on staff."

"You got no copies?"

"I didn't get around to doing it myself, and I didn't want to let anyone else do it."

"Shit, man."

"I know, I know. I fucked up."

"Where'd they get stolen from?"

Khalid points to a closet door. "It had a handle lock and padlock."

"You know that ain't going to keep no pro out."

"I know, man!" Khalid says, defensively. "I guess I just felt like the building itself was secure."

"Was it the FBI who did it?"

"I don't think so, because I can still push the Director's buttons. Same with the Mayor. That was my first thought, that one of them did it."

"The FBI could pull it off pretty easy. And the Mayor's got police aides who know how to break into places."

"But this happened more than three months ago, and no one's given any sign that I don't still have power over them."

"Inside job, then."

"I know, I know."

"Done any asking around?"

"Haven't figured out how to do that without letting it be known that the tapes are missing. If no one knows, then it almost doesn't matter."

A light knock sounds on the door. Khalid calls out to come in. A middle-aged Hispanic woman enters with a cleaning cart.

"The maid," Khalid says. "Another one of our businesses. Office cleaning. We hire Latinos to do it, and we make the capitalist profit. Nothing wrong with capitalism. Makes the world go round. But the Latinos, they'll do this work cheaper and better than our own. We're too regal, you know."

"Uh-huh," Long says.

Khalid tells the woman to come back later.

"Yeah. Listen, hey," Long says. "What do you think of this Henry James thing?"

Khalid, of course, doesn't know that Henry James was Long's brother. Meanly, bitterly, he says, "That cocksucker. I don't know for sure that Ells wasn't backed up, and I don't like no black man getting killed by a white, but still, I tell you something, I'm glad to see him gone."

"Yeah, he was a dog-fuck," Long says, maintaining the pretense.

"He was. Always after the Mayor for dealing with us. Every single city contract we worked out, he investigated. He had some shit on us too. I know it was just a matter of time before he took us to the grand jury."

"How you know?"

"We got word on his staff. We know."

"I thought maybe we did him."

"I thought about it. *Real* hard. But no, that wasn't us."

"What about that boy?"

Khalid shakes his head. "Shit, man. Come on. That Ells motherfucker, he didn't let no child live."

"How you know Ells got him?"

"I don't, I don't. I just do. He had to. Had to be him. If it wasn't, then where's the boy? Huh? Nah, there's no chance he's alive. I don't think I could honestly say I care about what happened to some spoiled little rich kid punk son of Henry James and that *bitch* whore wife of his anyway."

Long shrugs.

"Could have been the FBI, though," Khalid says. "They hated Henry. Could have been them using LTC, which they got a lot of power over. They could have set Ells up to do this. That's my theory. The Director himself has told me that that Joan Price woman is on his ticket."

Khalid asks Long to eat with him at New Africa's newest business, an upscale restaurant. Leaving the office, Long sees the Hispanic cleaning woman. Thinks about Chavez. Thinks about the boy. Thinks about his mother and how he has no hope to give her.

11

KELLOGG: GO SEE THE MOTHER. The grandmother.

Passer: Mrs. James?

Kellogg: Yeah.

Passer: What about?

Kellogg: Everything. Find out what she knows about what her son was working on before he got killed. Find out what she thinks about how the police and FBI have been handling things. Charm her. Sympathize with her. About the press, too, and what assholes they've been. You know. Get her to trust you.

Passer: Uh-huh.

Kellogg: And ask her what she thinks about the missing boy. I got a hunch that if the kid's not dead, which he probably is, but if he isn't, then she's got him. Not with her, but somewhere. With a relative or old friend. Maybe she's scared of the police. Maybe she's scared of LTC.

Passer: Maybe she's scared of the world.

Kellogg: Who could blame her?

Passer: Right.

Kellogg: But where else would the boy go, except to her house, if Ells didn't get him?

Passer: That's true.

Kellogg: Black up a little.

Passer: Why?

Kellogg: 'Cause you don't look half black as you are.

Passer: I'm not half black.

Kellogg: That's what I mean. Her grandkids are half black. You go in like that, it's an edge. The subtle bonding thing.

Passer: Is this my end?

Kellogg: I'm just saying.

Passer: Is this my end? My department?

Kellogg: All right.

They're in the coffee shop. He's eating a double hamburger with a full-plate side of fries. Passer is stealing his fries as they talk.

Passer: From what I heard, she doesn't talk to the press, the police, no one. Why should she talk to me?

Kellogg: I'm going to call her.

Passer: Oh, you're friends with her now?

Kellogg: We did that one job for Henry James, on that Chavez case. And for whatever reason, she was there every day. I talked to her once, in the hall, during a recess.

Passer: I did that case.

Kellogg: By yourself, almost. Because of your Spanish.

Passer: And I testified in that trial too. Which means she might remember me.

Kellogg: She'll definitely remember you by the time I'm done talking to her.

Passer: Uh-huh.

Kellogg: Stop eating my fries. I'll get you a plate if you want, but leave mine alone.

Passer, taking another fry, stuffs her mouth with it and asks: What's our official interest in her?

Kellogg: How about "A private individual has hired us to help find the boy"?

Passer: Fine.

Kellogg: Look around the house for signs the boy might be there. No, he won't be there, because he would have been seen. But see how worried she is. If she's cool about the assistance offer, it might just be because she knows he isn't missing.

Passer does "black up" a very little bit, with a lightly curled wig pulled over her own short, straight, fine hair; with some very slightly darkening foundation. Some accent and talk. Just a little. She's careful to underplay roles, but she knows Kellogg is right when he says people are more open with members of their own race. She knows the different prejudices about darkness within the black community. She could have, and has previously, blacked all the way up. But she thinks it's better psychology to go for the mixed-race look here.

She dresses sharply, professionally, in a navy-blue skirt with a white blouse, matching jacket, handbag, and pumps. As she stands at the corner during lunch hour on this bright spring day, flagging a cab, every man looks at her; most women do too. She's the picture of city confidence, youthful assurance, daytime elegance. She gets a cab in forty-five seconds. Minutes later she's at Mrs. James's dull-red brick row house, going up the steps of the wood porch, knocking on the door.

Mrs. James opens the door. Looks at Passer. Nods and smiles.

Passer, in sunglasses, seems arrogant, aloof, with her slenderness and height and style. She takes the sunglasses off, and the intelligent innocence of her eyes dispels the intimidation her beauty sometimes causes.

"I'm Catherine Jones," she says softly.

"I know," Mrs. James says, beckoning Passer inside, leading her down the wood-floored hall to the bright, daylit, white-tiled kitchen. "I remember you from your testimony at the Chavez trial."

"My boss, Kellogg, called you?"

"Yes."

They enter the kitchen, and Passer sees a light-skinned young girl whose stiff long hair is pulled back into a ponytail. Sitting at the table, she is drawing with colored markers. The girl looks up at Passer. Studies her. Doesn't speak.

Passer says hello and smiles. The girl, eyes running over Passer's clothes, says hello back but doesn't smile.

"This is my granddaughter," Mrs. James says.

"I gathered," Passer says. "She's so pretty."

"Isn't she? Interracial children just always seem better-looking than either parent. Isn't that strange? I always thought that was God's way of telling us something." She hesitates, then says, "Don't get mad I ask this, but what all is in you?"

"I don't mind you ask."

"Some people are sensitive about that question."

"I'm sensitive about it sometimes. But not paranoid. I'm part black, part Vietnamese, part Mexican, part white. My Vietnamese part is also half Chinese."

"That's a lot of stuff!" the little girl says.

Passer smiles. "I'm an all-American mongrel."

"No, not mongrel," Mrs. James says. "Thoroughbred."

"Okay," Passer says.

"You want some tea or coffee or soda?" Mrs. James asks.

"Sure. Whatever you have."

"Well, since we all went to England a few years ago, I have just loved a nice afternoon tea."

"Sounds good."

"It'll take a minute. You sit on down."

Passer sits by the girl while Mrs. James puts water on to boil, then pulls out a fine china tea service.

"This was my London souvenir," she says proudly, putting the cups and saucers and teapot, the creamer and sugar bowl, on the table.

"It's beautiful," Passer says, picking up a cup, examining it, admiring it.

"Are we going to have those cookies now?" the girl asks.

"Yes," Mrs. James declares. She takes a wondrously decorated tin box of cookies out of a cupboard, sets a lace napkin over a plate that matches the rest of the service, puts the cookies on the plate, and sets the plate on the table across from the girl, out of her reach. The girl says nothing, just bites her lower lip a bit.

"I think you'll survive five minutes of waiting," Passer says to her.

The girl looks forlornly at her coloring paper, sullenly

picks up a marker, and goes back to it. Passer and Mrs. James share a smile.

While the water comes to a boil, and then for a few minutes afterward as the tea steeps, Mrs. James and Passer talk about the neighborhood, her garden, tea, England. Passer tells a joke in perfectly mimicked British and Cockney accents, making the girl and Mrs. James laugh, relax. The tea comes ready and the cookie plate gets passed around. Ten minutes later the cookies are gone, the first cups of tea finished. The girl asks Passer to do her accents again, tell the joke again, which Passer does. After she stops laughing at Passer's joke, she asks, "Is that a wig?"

"Girl," Mrs. James says.

Passer pries into her hair, unzips the wig, and says, "You want to try it on?"

"Yes! I can? Cool."

She takes the wig and leads Passer to the bathroom, where Passer puts it on for her, as best she can considering it's big for the child's head. Passer then brushes up her own hair, washes her hands.

The girl shows off for her grandmother, asks if she can wear it until Ms. Jones leaves. Mrs. James says yes, but go outside, out back, and play in the garden, because they have to talk about some grown-up things. The girl's smile disappears. She knows what "grown-up things" means these days.

She turns on the radio on the windowsill. Points it outside so she can listen to it out there. Country music. Goes outside.

"She likes country music?" Passer asks.

"Her mother played it at home. I guess it soothes her now."

Mrs. James refills their teacups. Sits back down, across from Passer at the table, where she can keep an eye on her granddaughter. "Henry told me you made yourself look blacker for your testimony in the Chavez trial, to help with the jury. Is this your natural color now?"

"I'm a little lighter than this, even. I'm sorry."

"I don't mind. Henry said it was his idea to put you on the stand. That you didn't really need to testify, but he wanted you up there for just a minute, to help make the case seem more racially balanced."

A Washington Hispanic business organization had hired Passer to supplement what they considered a disappointing police investigation in that case, particularly within the Hispanic community.

"Did you talk much with your son about his cases?" Passer asks.

"No."

"Do you know what he was working on . . . last?"

Mrs. James sighs. "You work for Mr. Kellogg?"

"Yes."

"For what client?"

"That's private."

"So am I."

There's an edge in Mrs. James's voice when she says that. Part of her might sometimes fear the world, but part of her has lost too much to care too much. She could not have asked for more in a son, or been prouder than she'd been of Henry. She had come to truly love Jessica.

"Jimmy Close hired us."

"Hmm."

"You know who he is?"

"Yes."

"Does it offend you that we're working for him?"

"I don't know. *Why* are you working for him?"

"Mrs. James, Jimmy Close says LTC had nothing to do with your son and his wife's murder, or your grandson's disappearance. He told us that. He hired us, among other things, to help prove it. I believe him, by instinct."

"What does that have to do with me?"

"I don't know."

"What did you want to ask me about?"

"What can you tell us about your son's cases, his investigations, into the Mayor's administration, or New Africa, or any other political organization?"

"Nothing. He didn't mind if I sat in on the trials he prosecuted. But he didn't talk about his business with me."

"Do you think he knew Ells, even slightly?"

"I don't know. The police say they've found no connection."

"What about the boy? Any idea where he might be?"

She shakes her head, her shoulders droop. "I don't know."

Passer knows then that Mrs. James doesn't have the boy or know where he is. "Is there anyplace, or anyone, he might have gone to?"

"I've answered those questions for the police and the FBI."

"But you don't trust them."

"And I do trust you?"

"Yes."

Mrs. James smiles at the young woman's confidence and perceptiveness. Says, "Maybe."

Passer returns her smile. "My boss and I, between us, know this city, its people, and can get in anywhere and ask anyone anything. Better than the police, because we aren't the police. Let us look for the boy."

Mrs. James thinks about that. Says, "Of course. Maybe that would be good."

"So you still have hope for him?"

Tears suddenly rush down the older woman's face, and Passer cringes in recognition of her question's stupidity. She blinks back her own tears. Says, strongly, because she feels it strongly, "We're going to look for him. Okay? I swear to you."

Passer stares into Mrs. James's eyes. Asks, "What do you know that you haven't told the police?"

Mrs. James shakes her head. She fluctuates between great strength and determination, and weakness, surrender. The emotional switching exhausts her. "I think I do trust you. I need to trust someone. But my other son, he says don't trust anyone, don't talk to anyone."

"What?"

Mrs. James nods. "There is one thing I haven't told the police. And my other son, he's tried to look into it and not gotten anywhere. So I'd like you to look into it, because, for reasons you'll understand when I tell you, you're more likely than anyone to succeed at it. But I have to talk to my son first. Okay? Can you come back tonight?"

Passer nods.

"And bring your boss with you?"

12

LONG RAY SITS IN HIS MOTHER'S KITCHEN, saying no to the tea she's willing to make for him, saying he'll walk the few blocks to the store and get some black coffee. Says he'll think about what she's said. Says she might be right, but he still doesn't like it. Admits he can't get hold of Chavez but says working with white people always turns out bad.

She says, As opposed to all the associating you've done with blacks, which has put you in prison for most of your life?

Long walks to the store. Gets his coffee. Comes back. Turns off the porch light and sits outside, in a corner, nearly invisible in the dark, from which he can see the street.

Kellogg and Passer, driving his ex-taxi, park down the block in the only spot open this time of night. Kellogg labors up the walk. Passer slows down to not distance him, but bounds up the steps to the front door without him. She looks back. He's not following her; he's looking to the porch's corner. Saying, "How you doing?"

Only now does Passer notice Long, who's partly hidden from her by the front window's open shutter.

"You the man, huh?" Long says sarcastically.

Kellogg slowly climbs the three steps.

"You all right?" Long says. "That's three whole steps there."

"Don't worry about it."

"Why would I?"

"You the serial killer?"

"Don't worry about it."

"I got your sheet. Killed three people. And that's just the ones you been caught for." Kellogg, the find-it-out wizard, this afternoon made the calls, did the research, and learned who Mrs. James's other son must be, and then he made some calls and got his arrest record.

Long rises from his seat; glowers at Kellogg. Kellogg stands there, not the least intimidated. Passer sighs. Opens the door. Enters. The men follow her.

In the kitchen, Mrs. James has everyone sit around the table. The girl is upstairs sleeping.

Kellogg, polite, sincere, sensitive to Mrs. James's difficulties, says, "Ms. Jones tells me you want us to look for your grandson."

Mrs. James nods.

"She tells me you have some information about where he might have gone?"

Mrs. James nods again.

"Information you haven't told the police?"

Mrs. James nods one more time.

"Are you afraid of them?"

"I think Henry was working on some corruption investigation of them and the Mayor."

"Mrs. James," Kellogg says, "I don't think your grandson is alive. It's important to me not to mislead you at all. Not to give you any false hopes. But I admired Henry and would be happy to try to help."

She nods.

Long says, "You know, she don't trust the police, but I don't trust you. You're working for LTC, right?"

"Uh-huh."

"Those racist motherfuckers are the ones who killed my brother. Now they hire you to cover their own butts. And we're supposed to *trust* you?"

"If the path to the boy leads to LTC, I got no problem saying so."

"Just like that?"

"Sure."

Long sneers. Kellogg smiles, amused by him.

Passer asks, "Mrs. James, tell us what you know. Please?"

Mrs. James says, "You know Arcides Chavez. You did some work on that case."

Kellogg and Passer nod.

Mrs. James goes on. "Even though the men who killed Chavez's wife got off, Chavez respected Henry, and I think he did some work for him after that. I don't know what, but if Henry wasn't using the police, then I have to think it might somehow have had something to do with them."

She tells them the boy spoke of Chavez's working for Henry. She also tells about a night when she was at Henry and Jessica's house and Chavez came over. Henry and Chavez went into the den, shut the door, and stayed there a long time. And from Jessica, she gathered that it wasn't the first time Chavez had been there.

"And how does the boy connect with Chavez?" Kellogg asks.

"I remember—and his sister confirmed it when I asked her—that Chavez had become some kind of hero to the boy. Henry really respected Chavez, and you know the boy respected anyone Henry did. His father said that men like Chavez could be trusted long after others let you down. Henry told the boy that if things really got tough, if he ever got in real trouble, Chavez was the one he'd go to."

"Where is Arcides now?" Passer asks Kellogg.

Kellogg shakes his head. "I'm pretty sure he's moved out of the city. And I'm not sure how the boy could have gotten to him."

"Maybe he had his phone number," Mrs. James says. "I bet you he might have. But when I looked in the phone book and called the phone company, they didn't have him listed, here or in Maryland or Virginia."

"You didn't call from here, did you?" Kellogg asks.

Mrs. James looks confused by the question but answers with a negative shake of the head.

"I ask," Kellogg says, "because your line is probably being tapped."

"It is," she says. "The FBI said it would be, in case a ransom call came in. They asked me if they could."

"They would have anyway," Long says.

"They, or the police, might have been tapping it before all this, even," Kellogg says.

"But I called the phone company from a pay phone," Mrs. James says. "I wasn't thinking about a tap; I just happened to be taking my granddaughter for a walk, when she volunteered that maybe her brother had gone to Chavez, and I didn't want to wait to try to get hold of him."

"You know what Arcides might have been working on? For Henry?" Passer says. "Something to do with the riot."

A few years earlier, Latino residents rioted about a police shooting of a Latino man. Latino activists alleged, and police denied, that video footage of the incident existed, taped by a local television news reporter and crew, which proved that the victim was handcuffed at the time. The officer, a black woman, was cleared of the shooting. The television news reporter and his cameraman, both black, denied having a tape of the incident.

13

NEARLY TWO IN THE MORNING. Passer and Kellogg are at the diner. The cellular phone rings. Passer, expecting the call, answers. Speaks in Spanish. Hangs up. Says, "I didn't get an address, but I got the name of the bar he's working at in Georgetown. Dishwashing."

She tells Kellogg the bar's name. He knows it. Looks at his watch. Says Chavez should still be there.

Passer: They close at three?

Kellogg: At two. But dirty work stays late. Do this: Go get the car. Pull around to the back alley but don't stop, just go on through, up to the circle, then come back, stop at the front door, wait thirty seconds, then go around back to the alley entrance again and wait for me.

She knows this means he's worried about a tail.

Passer: Routine precaution or special reason?

Kellogg: Is there any chance Long or New Africa is

using us? They can't work in the Latino community. Long might have given us Arcides' name so we'd lead him there. I'm not saying that's the case but let's be aware of the possibility.

He takes a sip of coffee. Eats a mouth-filling bite of pie.

Passer goes through the routine with the car, and Kellogg, watching to see if anyone followed her, first when she pulled through the back alley and then when she faked the front-side parking job, sees nothing. She says she's seen nothing. Downtown D.C. is deserted this time of night. It's a bad time and place to tail anyone wary.

They drive to Georgetown in Kellogg's fake cab. Check the bar's front door—it's locked, the place just closed. They drive around and park in the alley behind the bar.

A half hour later they see Chavez come out with two large garbage bags. He's wearing a stained white apron over a sweatshirt and jeans. He puts the bags in the Dumpster and goes back in.

Another fifteen minutes go by.

Chavez, without the apron, comes out with another bag of garbage, throws it in the Dumpster, and starts up the alley in the other direction. Kellogg opens the car door and calls out, "Yo."

Chavez turns, eyes flaring. He squints.

Kellogg: Arcides, it's me.

Passer also calls out.

Chavez relaxes. Walks over to them. He smiles. Shakes hands with the still seated Kellogg. Chavez bends down, looks across Kellogg to Passer, smiles and says hola! Passer smiles broadly. She and Kellogg both like Chavez. Respect him. He is a short, wiry man with a proud mane of black hair, brown skin, sharp European features. His eyes seem always sad, never afraid.

Kellogg: Arcides, can we talk?

Chavez speaks English fairly well. He likes it that Passer speaks Spanish and that Kellogg hired her and trusts her; that helps him trust Kellogg. He is aware of prejudice the way most people are of weather. He knows what it is, occasionally behaves differently as it changes, but doesn't take it personally. As a boy, he had a gun in his hand, fighting the class war in El Salvador.

Chavez: You can take me home. I am in Arlington now.

He gets in the back seat. Passer drives. Kellogg turns in his seat as best he can, to look around at Chavez.

Kellogg: Hungry?

Chavez: No. I eat for free here.

Kellogg: Then I'll get to it. Arcides, what can you tell me about the murder of Henry James?

Chavez: Nothing. What I read in the paper.

Kellogg: You were working with Henry on something?

Chavez looks at Kellogg but says nothing.

Kellogg: Arcides, let me explain. The boy has not been found. We're looking for him. His grandmother said he might have gone to you.

Chavez, nodding: Now I understand, yes. One night, I told the boy that I had been a soldier and learned how to live with fear, and he asked if he could come to me if he was in trouble and I said of course. But it was nothing more than that. I had met with his father that night, at his house, and the son, he had been listening. He was in the den to get jelly beans from the jar Mr. James keeps on his desk there, and when we came in, he hid behind the couch. Mr. James later went to the bathroom. I heard a noise and found the boy. He was scared by what he heard us talk about. I said do not be scared. We had a talk. He was a good boy.

Passer, listening as she drives, asks: Arcides, did he know where you live?

Chavez: No, I do not think so. I had already moved to Arlington by then.

Kellogg: What were you and Henry talking about, that scared the boy?

Chavez: Kellogg, my friend, I trust you. But I have people to protect. And, even, you to protect. You are looking for the boy? I cannot help you.

Passer: He might have gone looking for you, Arcides.

Chavez: It hurts me, what happened. You know, Mr. James and I, we became very close. We thought the same way about things. I have come to understand in myself, and to see sometimes in others, what I call the dignity of patience. The pride that says no one can make me hate them. No matter what you do, I will not hate you. I will fight you, but I will not hate you. I will not hate you back. Mr. James, he understood this. He had this dignity. We talked about it. About the nature of hate. He was like my brother.

Chavez's voice is pained, his eyes narrowed.

Chavez: I would do anything to help the boy. You must know this is true.

They drive on in silence and shortly come to Chavez's apartment building, a red-brick three-story in a passable complex. Kellogg gives him a business card. Asks him to call if he thinks of anything.

✳

Kellogg and Passer go back to the diner/office. Have more coffee. They are opposites in many obvious ways, but they share a night owl habit.

For a half hour, they don't talk much, lost in their own thoughts.

Passer rubs her temples, sighs heavily. Says: I'm not happy.

Kellogg smiles and she does too.

Kellogg: Let's refocus.

Passer: Henry and Jessie James get killed by Richard Ells, who gets killed by Detective Mallory. There's no doubt that Ells killed the Jameses, or that he did it alone, because of the videotape. Ells has no concrete links to LTC except for a single attendance at one of their meetings, where he signed in on the guest sheet and left a motel's phone number.

Kellogg: LTC denies he had any involvement beyond that, and the media horde that went looking found nothing except LTC members irate over the media horde's looking.

Passer: Jimmy Close hires us to conduct our own investigation. Most specifically, he's worried about some videotape he expects Henry James to have but isn't sure he has, or where he has it if he does. Whether this tape is good or bad for Jimmy Close we don't know. But we do know that there might be some other videotapes in this town that are pretty dangerous, and therefore scary, to some pretty important people. And we know the boy wasn't killed at the scene, and disappeared with four videotapes.

Passer stops. Hesitates. Then goes on: It's funny how it just hits me sometimes, out of the blue, that there's this child out there somewhere, dead, or kidnapped, or just lost and wandering, in shock.

Kellogg: How can he be lost? How can he be wandering around? It's been three days. His picture's been on television and in the papers. The police did massive grid searching. Passer, get it out of your head that the boy's alive. He can't be. Even if no one outside the house, working with Ells, or Ells himself, killed the boy, then the boy, in some godawful shock, died on his own.

Passer: Then where's his body?

Kellogg: Rock Creek Park's a big place.

Passer: Not that big.

Kellogg: The Potomac River is. And maybe Ells killed the boy, took his body somewhere, came back to the James house for some reason, got himself killed. Maybe Ells didn't kill the boy. Just kidnapped him. The boy's dead now anyway, probably, if Ells stashed him somewhere secret, without food or water.

Passer: You can go three days without food. If he's got water, he's all right.

Kellogg: No. Not in the shock he must have been in.

Passer shakes her head.

Kellogg: Shape up, Pass. Quit hoping. If he is alive and gets found, then fine, we'll be all that much happier for the miracle. But he's not alive. Because no one who might have taken him, no one working with Ells, or Ells himself, would have any reason to keep him alive, and they'd have plenty of reason to kill him. Understand?

Passer nods.

Kellogg, compassionately: I'm sorry.

Passer nods again. She knows he is.

Kellogg: Maybe Ells did lock him up somewhere.

Passer: Locked him up and came back? Mallory shot him just a block away.

Kellogg: Criminals, especially mentally fucked ones, do come back to the crime scene sometimes. They get a thrill out of it. Especially someone like Ells. I mean, he taped the murders. That tells you something.

Passer: He had blood on his clothes. He wouldn't change first? Time of death was just after ten at night. Crime scene gets discovered at six the next morning. Ells gets shot about seven.

Kellogg: He didn't have that much blood on his clothes. And you're attributing logical behavior to a psycho.

Passer: Notice how we switch roles all the time? It's like we just naturally contradict each other.

Kellogg: I'm just thinking things through. The boy leaves, just after Ells. Ells grabs him. Takes him somewhere.

Passer: He isn't going to drive through the city, a white man with a screaming black child. He's going to put the boy in the trunk.

Kellogg: That was my original thought.

Passer: So if Ells didn't kill the boy, he locked him up, and the fact that no one's found him means the boy is still locked up, and if the shock didn't kill him, time has.

Kellogg, in a rare act, takes Passer's hand.

Kellogg: There's something about this case touching you real deep.

Passer: That boy, he could be my brother. Mixed-race child. You know?

Kellogg nods. Then, realizing where he'd put it, takes his hand away.

Passer: So he's almost certainly dead, and if he's not, he's hungry and terrified and in shock.

Kellogg: Passer, he has to be dead. If Chavez or Mrs. James didn't get him, then that only leaves the bad guys. And I trust my instincts that Chavez and Mrs. James told us the truth.

She nods. Accepts.

Passer: So what are we investigating? The police have nothing to go on, and no reason not to accept Ells as a sole actor, and aren't pushing any possible LTC connection. You're pretty sure they don't have the tape Close is worried about. So we don't really have an excuse to be involved in this. We should be getting started on investigating Joan Price. That was the other thing Jimmy Close wanted from us.

Kellogg: We'll be doing that soon. There's going to be an LTC fund-raiser in Rockville tomorrow. But we can justify looking for the boy because there's a good chance he's got the videotape of Henry James and Jimmy Close's meeting. Which brings us to the Big Fact. There's one in every case.

Passer: And the Big Fact here is?

Kellogg: The erasures on the Ells tape. Why would someone not want the world to know that the boy took videotapes with him?

Passer: It really could have been an accidental erasure. You're the one always saying never underestimate the role of chance in the world, never conclude conspiracy when incompetence or stupidity explains things just as well.

Kellogg: Nah, not here. It's too conspicuous. No, it all comes down to videotapes. Figure it this way: Henry James gets hold of some tapes. Part of some investigation. Major evidence. Keeps them at home instead of the office because he isn't ready to make it official yet, or he doesn't trust his office staff. He takes them home, hides them in boxes labeled as children's movies. Henry is his son's greatest hero, and the boy is fascinated with his work, completely loyal to him. The boy listens in on his father's conversations, like the one with Chavez. Learns about the videotapes' importance. Probably doesn't know anything but learns that they're important somehow. It all blows up in the boy's mind that his father's work is the most important work in the world and the tapes are the key.

The boy is sleeping. Gets woken by a noise. Goes downstairs. Finds his parents unbelievably butchered. In his mind, this is an attack on his father for what he stood for. And all that's left of what his father stood for is the video-tapes. I'm not saying the boy is thinking straight. Of course he isn't thinking straight. He's emotionally destroyed and clings to something, anything. To his father's work. To the tapes. He grabs them. Runs out. Maybe Ells gets him. Takes the boy and the tapes somewhere, kills him, locks him away, with the tapes. Maybe Ells in fact comes back to the crime scene hoping it hasn't been discovered and planning to go back in the house and get his own tape. Maybe, if Ells was working with people, those people got the boy and the tapes. Maybe it was the tapes they were after the whole time. The tapes, and the elimination of Henry James because he knew about the tapes. And then again, maybe the boy just runs and runs and collapses, or hides and collapses, and dies in some hidden place—some bridge underpass, some thicket in a patch of woods, some basement in an abandoned building.

Passer: Which brings us back to the Big Fact. The after-the-murder fact. The fact that someone with power or connections in the police department didn't want the fact of the tapes to be public knowledge.

Kellogg: We're saying tapes, plural, but it was probably just one tape that mattered to them.

Passer: So who has that kind of power with the police department?

Kellogg: New Africa, maybe. The FBI maybe. The Mayor, definitely. The police hierarchy itself.

Passer: But LTC, definitely not.

Kellogg: Definitely not.

Passer: And Mallory?

Kellogg: I'm surprised I haven't called him yet.

Passer: Do it.

Kellogg: Yessa, bozz.

Passer gets up, goes behind the diner counter, gets the coffeepot, pours Kellogg a refill but not herself, returns the pot, comes back.

Kellogg: By that I presume you're going to sleep soon.

Passer nods.

Kellogg lights a cigarette. Inhales, exhales, inhales, exhales. Thinks. Says: Chavez.

Passer: He knows something.

Kellogg: Not about the boy but about Henry James's investigations. They were working on something. Something—how did Chavez put it?—that we shouldn't know about for our own protection.

Passer: Yeah.

Kellogg: Chavez is not the sort to talk much, even to

people he trusts, assuming he trusts us. But we need to know what he knows.

Passer knocks on the table, points her finger at Kellogg. Says: Chavez is about family. He's sensitive about loss of family. That's our in.

Kellogg: How do we work it?

Passer: We get Mrs. James to personally ask him to help us.

Kellogg knocks on the table, too, in appreciation of the psychology Passer's figuring. He smiles. Says: You're right. That's our in with him. That's what he'll go for. A mother who's lost a son, asking him a favor.

Passer: And our interest?

Kellogg: Doing our job for Close, trying to track down the videotape he's worried about.

14

MRS. JAMES CALLS CHAVEZ. He remembers her from the trial of the men who murdered his wife, and respects her as Henry's mother, and sympathizes with her loss of family, and when she asks him to help Kellogg, he says of course he will. Thirty seconds after they hang up, his phone rings again. It's Kellogg, asking if they can meet. Chavez says he isn't working that day and that Kellogg can find him at a certain bar in Mount Pleasant, Washington's Hispanic neighborhood.

That afternoon, Passer, looking Latina, picks Kellogg up. They find the bar, park a block away, and walk up. The neighborhood, a commercial street surrounded by old but sometimes still attractive row houses and apartment buildings, bears scars from the riots but doesn't reek of despair, certainly not of danger. The streets are lively on this pretty, warm day, mostly with immigrant Latinos, but also with Americans. Everyone hanging out on the street is Latino. The two beat police are black, and they are eyed carefully, angrily.

The bar is busy but not overly crowded. Latin jazz plays softly. Passer instinctively moves with it as she leads Kellogg down the narrow aisle to an empty back table. Almost all the bar's patrons are men; almost all turn to look at her as she moves by them, her long legs in tight designer jeans balanced easily on black heels, her dark eyes in a heavily made up face sparkling out at them from under a brunette wig. Kellogg, too, is noticed, but for other reasons. He is the biggest man in the place. The whitest.

They sit. A waitress comes up and, curious as to whether Passer is Hispanic (enough Americans come in that she doesn't jump to that conclusion just because someone is dark), asks her in Spanish what they would like. Passer, in northern-Mexico-accented Spanish, answers they would like beer.

When the waitress leaves, Passer asks Kellogg if Chavez might not come. Kellogg says he would bet that he'd be here shortly, because when they came in, a man at the bar eyed them and then went straight to the phone and called someone.

Their beers come, with burning-hot salsa and chips.

"Why are you doing the Latina bit?" Kellogg asks.

"Just for fun. I miss it."

"Is that the main culture you grew up with?"

"Outside the house it was, when I was a teenager, because I was in a Mexican street gang. That's just one kind of Hispanic-American culture, of course. Just one part of it. Which is true of all cultures. People talk about what's a certain cultural characteristic, but really it's bullshit. There're so many ways to act like a 'kind' of person. But yeah, there are stereotypes, generalities, and I know how to use them. It's mostly just dress and attitude and accent, more than skin color. Really, I don't have to change my color at all if I don't want to. I mean, there are black Latinos, white Latinos, brown ones. Light-skinned black people, dark-skinned whites."

"You can do them all."

"Sure. And the world reacts differently to me too, depending on how I'm posing. And not just the white world. I find that blacks are the most color conscious, Latinos the least, whites somewhere in the middle. Latinos are the most class conscious, though, and blacks the least."

Kellogg laughs. "You should have been a cop. You are the most observant person I know. You dissect people's appearances and mannerisms and accents, see the patterns of what those things mean about who the person is. And what's more, you can mimic them."

"I could never be a cop."

"Why?"

"I'm too afraid of violence."

"Then go to college. Be a sociologist."

"I thought about it. But I can't fill out the admission forms. Right after name and address, they ask your race. Besides, I'm going to be a writer, remember?"

Chavez suddenly comes through the kitchen door and quickly sits with them. In his slight accent, he says, "You have Mrs. James call me for you. Very nice."

Kellogg is glad Chavez has a little humor in his voice. He has some in his own when he answers that he thought it was fair to remind him why they're on this investigation.

Chavez nods. "We will talk out back."

✳

In the alley behind the bar, Kellogg sits on a plastic milk crate, leaning back against the dirty white-brick wall.

Chavez sits on the black steel steps that lead to the heavy kitchen door, and Passer stands on the littered, puddled asphalt, hands in her pockets, looking for and seeing rats dodging about. Other restaurants' rear entrances feed this alley, and occasionally a busboy or dishwasher steps out with garbage to throw away. Once, three Latino boys come speeding by on their bikes, excited about something.

"Mr. James, he was a good man," Chavez says. "An honest man. And he helped me to live, to have reason to live, after the murder of my wife. I told him I *needed* to do something. So he asked me to do something for him. Something dangerous. He asked me because he knew I *had* to do something. I had to feel I was working to help things. I had dreams of taking my rifle against a gang and dying in battle. That gang, that crew, that killed my wife, that threatened the witnesses and scared them away from the truth, those men I could kill, those men could kill me, and I would not care. Mr. James, he gave me a chance to risk my life, to try, to do something dangerous, but to help.

"There is a man, Khalid. He has an organization, New Africa. You know of it?"

Passer and Kellogg nod.

"Mr. James, he heard, I do not know how, this New Africa had videos. Important videos. Videos of important people. And especially, for me, a video of the incident."

The "incident" is what the Latino community called the shooting of the local man by the black police officer that set off the riot.

"It showed, this video, it showed that our man was

handcuffed when they shot him. If we could get this video, it would mean much to our people. Mr. James said he believed New Africa had this video, and others—blackmail videos, he thought, maybe. But Mr. James could not trust the police to get this video, for obvious reasons. He went to the FBI, but they dismissed his claim. I think, in fact, Mr. James became afraid of them then. Of the FBI. He told me he was afraid all he had done, by going to them, was warn them that he knew something he should not.

"Mr. James, he tells me then he has an idea that I can get in the New Africa building, to get the tapes, by taking work as a janitor in the company that cleans the offices overnight.

"I know people in that company. I get the job. I am told by Mr. James where he believes the tapes are, and I find them there. I put them in a garbage bag and sneak them out of the building. I give them to Mr. James."

Kellogg lets a moment pass to be sure Chavez is finished volunteering information, then asks, "Did you watch the tapes?"

Chavez nods.

Kellogg lets another moment pass, then asks what was on them.

"One was of a white man who Mr. James said was the head of the FBI. He was doing things with a prostitute. That this was one of the tapes explains why Mr. James made a mistake in approaching the FBI about his suspicions about New Africa.

"Another tape was of the Mayor. He was in prison. He was in prison clothes, but he had a prostitute. A white woman. She did some things for him. And they smoked a crack pipe.

"And then there was a video of the incident. The man *was* handcuffed when the policewoman shot him. He was coming at her, and he was drunk, and he spit on her, and she drew her gun and shot him."

Passer asks, "What did Henry James say about that tape?"

"He said we should keep it for now and think about what to do. He said he was afraid that if the tape was made public it would just cause another riot. He said if I wanted, he would release the tape. He said it was my decision. But he asked me to consider whether the justice would be worth the violence."

"What did you decide?"

Chavez shakes his head. "Nothing. And now, of course, the tape is gone. I think the police must have gotten it back."

Kellogg: Did you or Henry James make copies of these tapes?

Chavez: I didn't. I don't think Henry did, because he said he had no place to safely keep a set of copies. We talked about maybe getting a safe-deposit box in someone else's name, but I don't think he had done that yet.

Kellogg: The police didn't get the tapes.

Chavez: How do you know?

Chavez assumed they did, because he knew they would have so thoroughly searched the James house after the murders.

Kellogg: I have a contact in the department. A good one.

Chavez: Then where are the tapes?

Kellogg: Whoever got the boy got the tapes. He took them with him.

Chavez nods again. His eyes water. He says: That boy, he loved his father. He loved what his father stood for. He would fight his father's fight.

A tear falls down Chavez's face. Passer notes how soft his light-brown skin is. Notes that she has not before really noticed his youth, because his eyes were always so hard-set, so aged. But Chavez is young. Not thirty.

Chavez: I know this boy.

He hesitates. Then: I was this boy. My father, he was a rebel. In El Salvador. As a boy, I saw him lead a company in the mountains. I saw him go off to fight, and come back. I saw the looks in the eyes of the other men in our town, heard the respect in their voices when they spoke of him. Of his courage.

One day, he was captured. And then a month later we woke up to find his naked body dumped in our town square. And you cannot know what had been done to him. You would not believe what had been done to him. But I will *never* forget what they had done to him.

All this, once, I told Mr. James. With his son listening, I told him. To help Mr. James understand what he was fighting. How universal is what he is fighting. How universal is corruption. His son, I'll tell you, that boy, he understood. And him *I* understand. I know where he is. Not where his body is. Where his heart is.

15

JOAN PRICE, FIVE THREE, STOCKY BUILD, permed hair, plain face, pale skin, dark eyes, dressed in slacks and blouse and heels bought at Sears, stands on a stage, microphone in hand, pacing. She has an energy that comes from absolute focus and a confidence that comes from absolute belief in her righteousness. She is speaking to a crowd of two hundred in Montgomery County, Maryland, which is a predominantly white suburb of D.C. and is one of the wealthiest, best-educated, and most liberal counties in the country. This is an LTC fund-raiser. Its very presence is controversial. People picket outside; burst in at one point and scream obscenities before being removed.

Jimmy Close is sitting on the stage. Watching Joan. He's thinking, of her, who is she? *Why* is she? He has his doubts about her. Worries about her. He knows what a fine line he's drawing with this movement. But he can't deny her talent. No one can. White Malcolm.

She is pacing. A plain-looking, middle-aged white woman of the sort most people find invisible in a crowd. She has a paper in her hand.

"This," she roars, to her white, Jewish, and Asian crowd, in this affluent suburb, "is the law."

She crumples the paper up, throws it away. Stands a moment, staring at her audience.

They stare back. In an age of medium-cool televised politicians with their studiously safe blandness, a live and real old-fashioned orator is fascinating. And she has the main asset of all great orators—she fakes nothing. She says nothing she doesn't believe. She says everything she does believe.

"The *law* says you cannot discriminate according to race."

She's a master of timing.

"The law says you can *not* discriminate according to race."

A master of inflection and emphasis.

"But the courts say that law means you *have* to discriminate. You *have* to. It's called affirmative action. Blacks said give us equal rights, and we did. Now they say give us superior rights, and we have. Our own children are second-class citizens in our own country. We don't just have government-tolerated hate, we now have government-mandated hate."

Jimmy Close, listening, watches the crowd. Joan Price is freelancing. Always does. Refuses to write a speech. Says you write letters, you *give* speeches. Says it has to be natural. Felt. Real. Emotional. If it's also unordered and inconsistent, so be it.

"The League of True Colors is an organization for poor

and working-class whites. Our people get proportionately less government help, suffer the worst media stereotypes, and have fewer educational opportunities than anyone else in America. Yet we aren't demanding quotas. We just don't want to be hurt by them. Blacks complain that their kids shouldn't have to study as hard as Asians and Jews but should get into college anyway; shouldn't have to work as hard at jobs but should get promoted anyway. You don't hear that from us."

She has a look and tone, for now, of conciliation. Her arms are spread wide, her hands are palm up.

"We are called racist."

She lets that statement sink in. She knows that her audience has heard the charge and is hurt by the charge.

"The media say that because we are against *black* racism, we are *ourselves* racist. Because we are *against* the hate-mongering of affirmative action, we are hatemongers? Wow!"

She says "Wow" in such a way that people laugh, caught off guard.

Now she changes pace. Begins stepping quickly about the stage, backward and forward, one side to the other, bobbing with her words, expressing with her arms, pointing with her hands, entrancing with a rhythm both verbal and visual.

"Things change fast in this modern, technological world. We read in the history books that there was a time when it was whites who were racist and blacks who were victims, but that was then, this is now. Now blacks are the bigots, not us. Not one white in a hundred is racist, not one black in a hundred isn't. Blacks who have never been oppressed get racial advantage. Whites, Asians, and Jews who have never oppressed are supposed to take their punishment with a smile."

It is no accident that she mentions Asians and Jews tonight. She understands the need for allies, for expansion. She wouldn't talk this way in Tennessee.

"Black politicians like to point out examples of individuals who've benefited from affirmative hate, but there were individuals who benefited from slavery too. Does that excuse it? The profiteers of bigotry cannot be their own argument.

"Black people have to understand that fairness isn't just something you have to demand; it's also something you have to give. Discrimination is wrong not only when you receive it but also when you dish it out.

"The problem is that black Americans have become a people of hate. Go see a movie made by blacks, watch a video made by blacks, listen to music made by blacks, read the lyrics. It's all about hate and violence. Black kids are brainwashed into thinking that we hate them. Brainwashed into interpreting our behavior as racist. Brainwashed into bigotry. Brainwashed into thinking violence against us is justified.

"Never mind that ninety-nine percent of all interracial crime in this country is *from* blacks *to* nonblacks. Never mind that more whites will die at the hands of black criminals this year than blacks were lynched by whites in a decade in the Old South. Never mind that one hundred percent of black economic inferiority comes from the fact that they are the worst parents in the world. Never mind that black people have *always* lagged behind everyone else in the world and that it *can't* have anything to do with racism because blacks were behind everyone else *before* whites came to Africa, which is how they ended up being bought for slaves in the *first* place. Never mind that Africans were the ones who invented slavery, and African chieftains sold their own people, and our European ancestors were the victims of the greatest con job in world history. Slavery was the worst thing to ever happen to this country. Africans sold Africans to Europeans, and centuries later their descendants are angry at *us*?"

That may have been the riskiest thing she will have said tonight, so by strategy she follows with her most powerful language:

"Never mind that my husband"—she chokes up, and the audience is completely silent—"was a good, open-minded man who believed we should stay in our neighborhood even though it had turned almost entirely black.

"Never mind that our daughter"—tears fall down her stern, angry face—"had a black girl for a best friend.

"Never mind what we do, or how we feel. When the time comes, when the blacks come, it doesn't matter how good we are. So many of us thought, if we were *good* whites, somehow we'd be protected."

Pause.

"Yet *every* day in *every* city in this country, blacks mug, murder, rob, and rape us."

She breathes deeply, passionately, loudly. Holds her hand to her temple and forehead, eyes closed a brief moment in concentration, collection. She opens her eyes, looks imploringly to her audience.

"How many people here have been victimized by black crime?"

Some hands go up.

"How many people have had loved ones victimized by black crime?"

Everyone's hand goes up.

"Then help us. Help the only true civil rights group in this country. Help us fight New Africa, the Nation of Islam, the N-double-hate-C-P, the Black Congressional Klan, and the other hate groups that are destroying this country. Help us save your lives."

Passer, looking her whitest, in jeans and boots, a ponytail wig under a ball cap, skin paled with makeup, and Kellogg, who's white as can be naturally, are in the audience, in the back.

Passer whispers to Kellogg, "She is awesome."

Kellogg nods.

Passer says, "I mean, I have never seen a woman speak like this. I'm not talking about right or wrong. I just mean, she can *speak*."

Kellogg nods again.

Jimmy Close called him today and suggested tonight as a good opportunity for Kellogg to begin investigating LTC. After all, the only provable connection between Richard Ells and LTC was Ells's attending a meeting such as this one.

After her speech, after an hour of talking with supporters, with reporters, with newcomers, Joan is finally alone, pouring herself a cup of coffee. Passer comes up to her. Speaks in a heavy New Orleans accent she learned during her stay there. Puts out her hand.

Passer: Mrs. Price? I'm Adelia Desormeaux.

Joan Price takes the proffered hand. Shakes it. Looks Passer in the eye.

Passer: Mrs. Price, I just have to say, my God, what you said all tonight, it is just something I have never heard so well before.

Joan: Thank you. Adelia Desormeaux?

Passer: Yes.

Joan: Thank you. We haven't seen you before, have we?

Passer: No, this is my first time, but I had to come, because I read about you in *Time* magazine, and then heard you speak on the radio, and saw you on Ricki Lake and Geraldo, and I just had to come.

Joan: Thank you. I hope that means you're going to get active in the movement.

Passer: Absolutely!

Joan: Great. Do you have any background in political activism?

Passer: Yes, I do. I worked on David Duke's campaign back home. It still hurts me we came up just short on that, but still, you know, we got some things said.

Joan: You're from Louisiana?

Passer: New Orleans.

Joan: I thought I recognized that accent.

Passer: Ain't much mistaking it for nothing around here.

Joan: No, there isn't. It's a great accent.

Passer: You never meet no one from home ever makes the least bit effort to talk like the rest of y'all.

Joan laughs.

Passer: Anyway, Mrs. Price, I just think what you say and do is so right, and I want to be a part of it. I came up here just for that. I want to work with you.

Joan: You came up here to work with me? Really?

Joan Price is still new to her own power. She still enjoys, like a revelation, hearing that people are moved by her speeches.

Passer: I got thirty-three hundred dollars to live on for a while, and I can stay rent free in Frederick with my uncle.

Passer points to Kellogg, who, across the room, his huge belly sprawling out from under a T-shirt, over his jeans, looks as much a redneck as anyone ever does. His T-shirt says PEOPLE WHO BELIEVE IN ABORTION SHOULD HAVE BEEN ONE.

Passer: Well, I don't mean to gush. Or keep you. I know you must be so busy, so many people demanding your time.

Joan Price smiles up at Passer. Asks if she's hungry. Passer says yes, very much so. Joan says, Come eat with me. Passer asks if her uncle can come too, and Joan says certainly.

Earlier this day, Passer and Kellogg went out to Frederick and borrowed a truck, with Maryland tags that can be traced to a Frederick address. The man who owns the truck is a retired police officer, an old friend of Kellogg's named Desormeaux with a daughter named Adelia, so they can get by a casual check, if Joan runs one.

16

NIGHT, AT THE TASTEE DINER IN BETHESDA. The temperature has dropped, and a slight rain falls, misting the windows. Joan Price has brought a tall, sharp-eyed young blond man who takes his job as her bodyguard very seriously. He sits with them all at the diner but doesn't join in the conversation much. Stares at Passer a lot.

The conversation at first is indirect. Passer, who's done some library research on the subject, speaks about the David Duke campaign; Joan Price is very interested. Passer says she answered phones in a New Orleans office for a month and did some leaflet distribution, and poll work on election day. She has actually done those things as a kid for one of Tom Bradley's mayoral campaigns in Los Angeles, so she feels comfortable discussing the work. And she has seen Duke speak on C-SPAN.

"You know what I remember most about the David Duke campaign?" Joan says. She's eaten amply and is drinking coffee. She doesn't smoke. "You know, blacks are always talking about redemption, but they aren't willing to give anyone else any. They say forgive the Mayor, forgive Tyson, forgive Farrakhan, but don't forgive David Duke. Tell me, Adelia, do you know anything about Malcolm X?"

Passer: I saw the movie.

Kellogg, who's been busy eating, says, "I tried to watch it when it was on cable, but I turned it off after about thirty seconds—as soon as that nigger started preaching that white-hating bullshit of his."

Joan, pointing her finger at Kellogg, sternly says, "We don't use that word. Period."

Kellogg: They use it. All the time.

Joan Price: I don't care. I don't use it, and I can't let people around me use it.

Kellogg shrugs his big shoulders.

Passer: It just gets us in trouble.

Price: Exactly. We have to be more careful about such things than anyone else. We are held to a higher standard. If we say we prefer vanilla ice cream to chocolate, we can be accused of racism. Getting back to Malcolm X, he is someone I understand very well, but with regard to David Duke, remember that Malcolm, too, at first said horrible things about whites, but we are supposed to overlook them because at the end of his life he started changing his views. He was still a separatist, as I am, but he realized the futility of hate. As I do.

Kellogg: And as soon as he stopped hating whites, the blacks killed him.

Price, nodding: That's true. And it's also true that blacks today idolize Malcolm because, as a young man, he was a racist fanatic. But understand, thirty years ago things were very different in this country. If you know history, you know there was a time in this country when it was whites who were the violent racists, whites who organized politically along racial lines, whites who got away with crimes if their victims were black, whites who got job preference so absolute that it makes affirmative action look like nothing. I always try to bear this in mind when I think about succumbing to my own anger.

Passer: I remember you said it's important not to let blacks drag us into the gutter of racial hate with them.

Price: That's right. You know, I used to be a liberal. People wonder why I'm so good at slicing liberal arguments. It's because I know those arguments so well. But now liberals are the status quo, which means they aren't really liberal at all. Empowered liberal whites still feel superior to others, but they've added poor and working-class whites to their list. Empowered whites are liberal only inasmuch as they're scared to say anything that can be construed as anti-black. Here's another thing I have in common with Malcolm—we both detest white liberals. In the same way he had more respect for the openly anti-black Southern whites of his time than he did for the Yankee phonies, I have more respect for black nationalists than I do for white liberals. In fact, I *agree* with black nationalists.

Passer: I know you agree with New Africa.

Price: New Africa is a great idea. African Americans are Americans. They've lived here for hundreds of years, fought and died in wars to keep us all free. They aren't Africans, they're African Americans. They have as much right to be here as anyone else. New Africa's idea of carving out a country for blacks is fine by me. I don't want to live with them anymore.

Kellogg: Me, neither.

Passer: Yeah.

Passer and Kellogg did some homework on Joan Price and LTC, and knew in advance the necessity of agreeing with the idea of New Africa.

Price: They say they want Georgia and South Carolina. It can be worked out. We can even give them, say, twenty billion a year for the first ten years, so they have some operating capital. Forgive them their share of the national debt—even though if it weren't for blacks there wouldn't *be* a national debt, because it's their failure to join the economic mainstream that is the cause of all our problems.

Kellogg: What if some blacks don't want to go?

Price, laughing: Well, you couldn't blame them, but even if only half go, that still cuts our black population in half. And whites who want to stay in Georgia and South Carolina I'm sure will be welcome, as long as they understand they're going to be in the minority.

Kellogg: The thing is, you know black people can't run their own government. Look at what they did to D.C. They can't run things.

Price: Of course. All the laws and hate quotas in the world can't change the fact of the bell curve. But as long as they're out of our hair, who cares? Think about how nice it would be not to have blacks around. Our schools would work again, because the disrupters would be gone. Our cities would be safe, which would free us to live with culture and civility like they do in Europe. Our tax rate would drop, because we wouldn't have so many millions of blacks to support. It's paradise. Of course New Africa would fail. Blacks have about as much chance of running their own country successfully as the Japanese have of winning a gold medal in basketball, and for the same reason. But that wouldn't be our concern. We separate from blacks. Give them their own country. Build a wall around it so they can't sneak back in here. And presto—paradise!

Kellogg: Sounds like a plan.

Price: And it's their plan too. Funny how I'm called a racist for agreeing with them. It's true, there is a part of me that wants revenge on blacks for what they've done to me, to us all. You know, Africans butchered, conquered, and enslaved Europeans for a thousand years. The Moors, the Arabs. What Asian Mongols did for centuries to whites in Russia was worse than anything we ever did to anyone. We've been terribly victimized by other races. In fact, blacks still owe us a few hundred years of servitude, as I see it. And reparations for the destruction their affirmative hate has caused us all these past decades, and their current genocidal crime war against us. But I'm willing to forgive and forget, as long as I don't have to live with them anymore.

Kellogg: Yeah. Who knows. Maybe if we go our separate ways, we could even be friends.

Price: For better or worse, we do have a long history together. It could be like a constantly fighting married couple who get along better after the divorce.

Passer: What about the Asians and the Mexicans? There's getting to be too many of them too.

Kellogg: And the Jews.

Passer: Yeah, and the Jews.

Price: They're all all right. It's just the blacks who can't get along with anyone else. They riot against Koreans in L.A., Cubans in Miami, Jews in New York. They're the problem. You know, the government did a study and found out that blacks were two and a half times as likely to get disciplined on the job than whites, Asians, or Latinos. Blacks are always saying it's a white racist society, but if we're so racist, how come Latinos and Asians don't get disciplined any more frequently than whites do? Face it, we aren't racist. Asians, Jews, Arabs, Latinos, they all do fine here. Even African immigrants do well here, so it isn't color. It's just black Americans who are failures, which proves it isn't us, it's them that's the problem. They're choking to death on their own bigotry, not ours.

Kellogg: But what can we do in the meantime? I mean, we *want* to do something.

Kellogg is eager to make it clear to Joan Price that he and Passer, in their role as the Desormeauxes, are willing to go beyond politics.

Price: Keep organizing. Which is hard, now, because the media are blasting us.

Passer: That's so unfair.

Kellogg: Blacks can join pro-black groups, but if we join pro-white groups we're cooked.

Passer: How come you don't talk like this more often in public?

Price, frowning: Jimmy Close. I'll tell you, to Jimmy, race is an idea, not a reality. Living up there in West Virginia, he doesn't know any blacks. He doesn't know what it's like to have your kids come home from school crying because some racist pig black was hitting them.

Passer, like Kellogg, keeps the point of this conversation, from their end, in mind and asks: But what *can* we do? I mean, really. What can we do? Just oppose affirmative action and stuff?

Price: For now.

Passer: It just doesn't seem like enough. Not when we're getting terrorized by black violence so much.

Kellogg: Hey—*never* give up your gun.

Price, nodding: That's true.

Passer, lowering her voice conspiratorially: Mrs. Price, we want to do more.

Kellogg nods in agreement. Leans forward.

Price looks at them carefully. Her bodyguard, who hasn't really been listening too much because he's heard all this so often before, perks up now.

Price: Listen very carefully. America is a *victim*-oriented society now. Okay? Do you know what that means? It means whoever can paint themselves as the most victimized gets the most public support. That's why I've been so successful. I *am* a victim. I don't have to fake my tears, I have to control them. But if we attack back, even in self-defense, we lose public support. I understand the Oklahoma City bombing, for example. In a way. I mean, what the government did at Waco was horrifying. But by blowing up that building, the militias just hurt themselves. They even hurt us a little.

Kellogg: Like that Richard Ells killer? Was he with you all? I guess you wouldn't tell us.

Price: I'll tell you. I met him. I remember him. I meet a

lot of people, but I remember him because he acted funny. Very funny. Acted like he was up to something. Personally, I think somebody wanted to frame us for the murders, or at least make us look bad by association, and so they maybe brought him out to a meeting just to establish a little bit of a connection and get him some of our pamphlets.

Kellogg: I remember the *Washington Post* jumped at the chance to blame you.

Price: That paper's done everything it can to hurt us. Fortunately, most people know what a diseased, self-hating bunch of white Uncle Toms are running it. Just like Malcolm most hated the Uncle Tom appeasers of his day, I most hate the Uncle Toms we have. The whites who fear blacks. Who say, basically, let's give them money and job preference so they won't riot. So they'll like us.

Kellogg: Nothing I hate more than nigger-scared white people.

The blond bodyguard laughs. Nods agreement.

Price: I warned you about using that word, sir.

Kellogg: Okay, okay.

Passer: So you're saying, really, we can't fight back? I mean, take the fight to them? With all they're doing to us?

Price: No. No violence. Violence is a black thing. When you meet a snake in the grass, do you get down on your belly and hiss? If you meet a rat in an alley, do you scurry on all fours and try to bite it? If you meet a bear in the woods, do you roar and grapple with him? Of course not. So when you meet a black, you don't fight him. God gave the black man muscles; he gave us brains. I do believe in self-defense, but we can do this politically. We just have to mobilize the anger. The best revenge on blacks is to let them have their own country. Imagine how much fun it's going to be, watching it become Somalia.

Passer: I guess. I just, you know, want to do more.

Kellogg: To tell you the truth, we came here hoping you could help us. See, I know security systems. I can get us into any building, just about. And Adelia, well, let me tell you, this Cajun girl can *shoot*!

Passer smiles shyly. The bodyguard, who is quickly developing a crush on her, smiles broadly.

Price: No, no. If we do that, we're playing into their hands. Listen, the whole thing is to just unite ourselves and make ourselves scarier, as a race, to blacks, so that they feel more justified in their bigotry, more justified in their hate, and more justified in their claim for separation. And part of the way we do that is to oppose things like affirmative action. Affirmative action really isn't very harmful to us. It is disgusting on principle, as discrimination always is, but there aren't really that many of us losing that much because of it. I hate it mostly because it isn't applied to the empowered class of whites who are the same sons-of-bitches who benefited from the discrimination it's supposed to be making up for. But the thing about affirmative action is, it's symbolic. And opposing it makes them feel hated. It makes them scared. And the more fear they have, the more anger they express, and the more violence they commit, and then the more truth we have to work with. Don't you see the genius of my plan? I'm going to use black people's sickness to destroy them. I can't wait for them to get their own country. I can't wait for their own police to have to try to control their sick young males. I can't wait to see them starve because they won't have Whitey to do their farming for them. I mean, who's going to fly their planes, build their houses, manage their power plants? No, we don't need violence to destroy them; we just need to give them what they want.

Kellogg and Passer drive out to Frederick to trade the truck back for her car, and to back up their role playing if anyone is tailing them. Kellogg has already taped a message on the answering machine at the real Desormeauxes' phone if someone calls.

Passer: You worry me, Kevin.

Kellogg: Always have.

Passer: You get into that white racist role too easily. I think you enjoy it.

Kellogg: Tomorrow that bodyguard of hers is going to call you. I gave him your number, our number, in Frederick. He'll leave a message, if he's intelligent enough to figure out how answering machines work. You call up there, get the message, call him back, go out with him.

Passer: You think he's a factor?

Kellogg: No. I think Joan Price is straight too. Obsessed, but considering what she's been through, who can blame her? But I think this kid would love to impress you. If he isn't really doing anything, if they aren't doing anything, if *she* isn't doing anything, he'll impress you with hot air. But if there is something going on, you'll flirt it out of him.

Passer: Easy for you to say.

They're passing exits on the freeway, wipers slapping through the foggy night. They stopped for coffee at a 7–Eleven. Passer finishes her eight-ounce cup at the same time Kellogg finishes his twenty-ouncer; finishes her second cigarette at the same time he finishes his sixth; finishes her only doughnut as he bites into his third.

"And no," Kellogg says, "I don't enjoy talking like I did tonight. But I like some of what she says."

"She's a racist, Kevin."

"Anyone saying anything blacks don't want to hear is racist. It's just a word used to shut whites up."

Passer sighs.

17

LONG RAY AND KHALID ARE IN KHALID'S GRAND OFFICE in the New Africa headquarters. They're watching a videotape of Joan Price's speech the night before.

Joan Price: In Malcolm X's autobiography, he writes the question, How can whites atone for brutalizing millions of humans over the centuries? What atonement could ever be enough?

We have nothing to atone for! Of what crime are we really guilty? Winning? Even if we say our ancestors committed crimes, what does that have to do with us? What sense does it make to punish a criminal's descendant? If your brother robs a bank, should we put *you* in jail? And when you consider that black Americans are the wealthiest, freest, best-educated, longest-living, and most powerful blacks in world history, *they* should thank *us*! Every day they don't wake up in Africa, they should thank us. But the egomaniacs can't admit it, so they twist history around to make it seem like *we* owe *them*!

Khalid laughs. Long smiles with him.

Khalid: She's good! I love her.

Long: She *is* good.

Khalid: Did you ever see her on television for that meeting with the guy who killed her husband and child?

Long: Where she really screamed at him?

Khalid: Screamed. Cried. The whole bit.

Long: Yeah, I saw it.

Khalid: As soon as I saw that, I knew she was the perfect foil. Exactly what we needed. Now listen to this.

He gets up, puts another tape in the VCR. Says: This woman is fascinating to me, really. And partly because she is herself so fascinated with Malcolm.

Price: Some have said that I am a segregationist. I am not. I am a separatist. As Malcolm X said, separation is something done voluntarily, for the good of both races. I agree with him. We whites can live with Asians, with Jews, with Latinos, with Arabs. But *not with blacks. Nobody* in world history has ever been able to live in peace, and prosperity, with blacks. Nobody. Ever.

Khalid fast-forwards on the tape. Says: This is my favorite part. Straight Malcolm. Check this out.

Joan Price: I charge the black man with being the greatest *murderer* on earth. The greatest *rapist* on earth. There is no place on this world that that man can go and say he brought peace and harmony. Everywhere he's gone, he's created havoc. Everywhere he's gone, he's created destruction. I charge him with being the greatest *drug*-abuser on this earth, the greatest *woman*-beater on this earth, the greatest *slave*-seller on this earth, the greatest *child*-leaver on this earth, the greatest *pimp* on this earth, the greatest *school*-destroyer on this earth, the greatest *con* artist. He can't deny the charges.

We don't have democracy in America, we have hypocrisy. Oh, I'll say, and I'll say it again, you've been lied to by the so-called civil rights movement. They were never against discrimination; they just wanted to dish it out instead of receive it. Black people lied to us. I'll say it again: You've been had.

Took.

Hoodwinked.

Bamboozled.

Led astray.

You know, some people call this hate-teaching. This isn't hate-teaching, this is love-teaching. I wouldn't tell you this if I didn't love you.

The black supremacists try to hide their guilt by accusing me of being a white supremacist, simply because I'm trying to uplift the mentality and social condition of my people.

We have been the victim of violence too long. You've got Uncle Tom whites who tell us we ought to love blacks, we ought to integrate with our enemy. But that wouldn't be intelligent. We have the right to defend ourselves. That's only natural. We're not saying hate the black man; we're saying love ourselves. Resistance is the secret of joy.

✳

Khalid is nodding his head in time with Joan Price's rhythm. Long is silent.

Khalid: Anyway, she's about to make a break with Jimmy Close, because he's too "reasonable."

Long: The FBI tell us that?

Khalid: Yep.

Long: What do you think of that?

Khalid: "Reasonable" is bullshit.

Long calls Kellogg Investigations. Leaves his number at the hotel, for Passer to call.

That afternoon, when she wakes and checks the office, she gets his message and calls.

Passer: Hey. What's up?

Long: Who's this?

Passer: Me. Passer.

Long: What's up?

Passer: I got your message.

Long: I want you to tell me the truth about LTC. I want to know what you know about them.

Passer: You want a trade? Info on LTC for info on New Africa?

Long, after a moment: Your boss will go for it.

Passer: He thinks New Africa, or the Mayor, or both, have something to do with all this. Theoretically I could get into New Africa, passing for black, and in time, a long time, find some things out. But I doubt it. Big-time decisions don't get spilled that easily to anyone, especially to newcomers.

Long: But I can find out anything at New Africa.

Passer: Yes.

Long: Okay.

Passer: Okay? Okay you'll investigate your own people?

Long: I don't need to investigate them. I can tell you straight, New Africa had nothing to do with my brother's murder, and I haven't heard nothing to implicate the Mayor, either. But I will keep asking questions, and if I find something, I'll be straight with you about it.

Passer: Okay. That's good enough.

Long: But if it's at LTC, if the truth is at LTC, would you tell me?

Passer, sensitive to such things, hears a change in Long's voice. Something's different.

Passer: What?

Long: You going to be straight with me?

Passer: Yes!

Long is silent.

Passer, again: What?

Long: I'm going to find that boy. You understand me? I ain't never done nothing my whole life for my mother. Just broke her heart over and over and over. But I'm telling you right now, *this* I can do. He's disappeared into the streets of this city? *Nobody* knows this city better than me. You understand? *Nobody*. And if that boy's out there, I'm going to find him. And I don't care who gets in my way. You understand, girl?

Now it's Passer who's silent. Wondering what happened; sensing something has.

That morning, at Mrs. James's house, when the mail came, her granddaughter got it. She looked through it absentmindedly, hoping only for a certain girls' magazine she subscribed to, then she saw a letter addressed to her. Excited, she started to open it, then remembered (because of all the hate mail the family had received) that she wasn't allowed to open mail until a grown-up checked it.

She took it downstairs to the basement, where her grandmother was doing laundry, and gave it to her.

Mrs. James, holding a box of detergent, looked at the handwriting and dropped the box. Hands shaking, tears welling, hope growing, she fumbled to open the letter. When she did and saw she was right, she gasped, and the tears fell—it was from her grandson. It said only: "I am okay. A nice man is taking care of me. Tell Grandmommy I am okay and will come home soon, if I think it is safe, but right now there are people watching her house and they might want to kill me, I don't know. I am trying to feel better. I am sorry about Mommy and Daddy."

Mrs. James called Long. Told him. Asked him what she should do. He said do nothing till he got there.

He came over. Read the letter. Again and again. Postmarked D.C.

Long Ray is very even-tempered, emotionless when it's called for. You can put a gun to his head and he won't blink; a knife to his throat and he won't gulp. It's what made him the leader he was in prison. Cool in the face of heat, calm in a storm of fear. But the reason he's always been so cool is that he often had trouble caring about even his own life, much less someone else's. A lifetime of brutality, and a sense of his superiority to his superiors, have laced him in cold anger and cheap pride. But this boy's handwriting made him feel something: the girl's need for hope. His mother's.

He went to Khalid to make a proposal.

Long: I've been thinking about that boy. The missing one.

Khalid: The James boy?

Long: Yeah.

Khalid: Why?

Long: I think it would be a great publicity move for us to look for him.

Khalid: What if we can't find him? What if he's dead, like he probably is?

Long: We still look good making the search. Remember the television coverage from Oklahoma City, and how good the reporters made the rescue workers look? We can do that here. We can say to the people that *we* are the ones who care. You admit we have a fine line to draw between our militancy and our compassion.

Khalid: And looking for the boy is both.

Long: Exactly.

Khalid: I don't know.

Long: It's a public case, but the press is off it. So we play that angle. "One of our own is missing, but the press and the law enforcement don't care because it's a black child."

Khalid: Yeah, that's good.

Long: We can make this big public demonstration. Sweep through the streets, going door to door, asking people if they've seen the boy or what they might know but been afraid to tell the police.

Khalid: And at the same time, we can be passing out

New Africa leaflets, showing the people how good we look, how disciplined we are. Yeah, okay, I like it. Of course, there's no chance we'll find the boy, but that's not important. Tell you what. We'll draw up a street-canvassing plan today and announce it at the rally tonight.

18

KELLOGG IS AT A TABLE IN DEJAZBA, whiskey in one hand, cigarette in the other, trumpet solo in his ears, when Mallory enters. Kellogg, always more alert than others might guess from his drooping head and sloppy dress, sees Mallory right away and waves him over.

Mallory sits. The waitress comes up. Mallory orders a beer, Kellogg another whiskey. The men sit silently until she returns with the drinks and leaves.

Mallory: Why do you like this place?

Kellogg: 'Cause I can get shit-faced in peace. Because I've been coming here so long I can find the pisser even when I'm blind drunk. Because the bartenders know to get me a cab home when it's time, and where home is for me. And because I like the music.

Mallory laughs. Shakes his head. Drinks his beer.

Kellogg: You took your time getting back to me.

Mallory: I don't work for you.

Kellogg: No, John, you don't.

Mallory: Relax, Kevin.

Kellogg: Let's get down to it.

Mallory: Why not.

Kellogg: Is there anything more to your shooting of Richard Ells than what's been made public?

Mallory: Nope.

Kellogg: You just happened to be there?

Mallory: No, I was called there. As was just about every other dick on the force.

Kellogg: You just happened to be in the alley where Ells was hanging around?

Mallory: I was auxiliary on this case. Never went in the house. Just got sent out for street canvassing. Went to look in the Dumpster because, as you know, perps often use them to get rid of stuff. In that alley, I saw Ells. That's all.

Kellogg: No it isn't.

Mallory: Fuck you it isn't.

Kellogg: He didn't say anything to you before you shot him?

Mallory: Nope.

Kellogg: Didn't have anything on him?

Mallory (sarcastically): Just a gun.

Kellogg: No videotapes?

Mallory: You got contacts on the force besides me.

Kellogg: Of course.

Mallory: Probably heard about the boy.

Kellogg: Of course.

Mallory: What?

Kellogg: That he took a bunch of tapes with him.

Mallory: What else?

Kellogg: That somebody in the department or the Mayor's office didn't want the fact of those tapes being taken, or maybe even existing, made public.

Mallory: Now, see, that I didn't know for sure. Heard rumors that the last half minute of the tape Ells made of the murder was erased, but I didn't know for sure.

Kellogg: What difference does it make to you?

Mallory: Not much. Curiosity.

Kellogg: When are you out?

Mallory: Now, effectively. Routine suspension, but after that I'm retiring.

Kellogg: Going where?

Mallory: West Virginia.

Kellogg: Conspicuous choice.

Mallory: I got nothing to do with LTC, if that's what you mean.

Kellogg: That's what I mean.

Mallory: I got nothing to do with them.

Kellogg: Why West Virginia?

Mallory: Maybe I like the fishing.

Kellogg: Maybe you'd just as soon never see another black face the rest of your life.

Mallory, after a deep sigh: You remember how we were? When we first came on the force?

Kellogg: We've had this conversation before.

Mallory: Remember how we used to think we'd be a new breed of cop? How we'd help people, black or white, equally? How we wouldn't be like the older cops, beating every nigger they came across?

Kellogg nods. Drinks his whiskey.

Mallory: Remember Wilson taking a bullet because he

didn't shoot fast enough himself, because he was so afraid of accidentally shooting a black man? Remember Smith going back into that burning building to try and save one more kid, only to never come out alive? Burned to death saving black kids who would grow up to hate his guts and kill him if they ever got the chance? Remember that ER nurse who dedicated her life to an inner-city hospital, only to be killed by two black girls in a carjacking? How often has that happened? How often have we risked our lives to save black people who wouldn't spit on us if we were on fire?

Kellogg: Drop it.

Mallory: I can remember the Mayor when he was first running for office saying white police were racist because we never believed anything black suspects told us. But I can also remember reading in Malcolm X's biography how stupid white cops were for believing his lies. You gave me that book.

Kellogg: You didn't finish it.

Mallory: I read enough. And by then I'd had a year of this city's streets and I knew enough. Like your hero Malcolm said, the Negro is a natural-born dissembler. And Negroes lie so much they can't even keep their lies straight themselves. You remember that?

Kellogg: I remember.

Mallory: We were suckers, Kevin. This whole nation is a sucker. White people are suckers. I tell you, brother, our ancestors knew blacks better than we did.

Kellogg: Ever talk to Ells about this?

Mallory: I never talked to Ells.

Kellogg: Think he agreed with you?

Mallory: I wouldn't know.

Kellogg: They found white supremacist pamphlets in that motel room he was living in. In West Virginia.

Mallory: They found all kinds of shit in his room. New Africa shit. NAACP shit. Democratic party shit. Republican party shit.

Kellogg: Did he have friends into anything?

Mallory: His only friends were other racetrack grooms, mostly older, drunken ones. Bunch of losers, just like him. They were interviewed. Said little about him, because they didn't know much about him, or want to know much, because he was weird. Not just a loser, like they all are, but weird. They were asked about his political beliefs. They all said when he was drunk he'd spout off, but no one could make sense of what he said. They couldn't even tell if he was a liberal or a conservative. He just seemed to hate at random. One black groom said he'd got trapped at a bar for an hour listening to Ells rant on about how he, the black guy, had to agree that no matter what else they disagreed about, *everyone* agreed race mixing was evil.

Kellogg: And no one ever drew a connection between LTC and Ells?

Mallory: I wasn't in the investigation, but of course I kept a close ear to it for my exoneration. But no, the investigating team never drew a connection between Ells and anyone. Not even the sniff of a connection. He was acting alone. That might not be fun to believe, but I think it's the truth. It's certainly the truth as I can figure it.

Kellogg: I believe you.

Mallory: I don't care. I don't care if you believe me, or if the department believes me, or if the public believes me. I'm done living a life where I have to be believed at all.

Kellogg: Yeah yeah yeah. What about the boy?

Mallory: Well, that is a mystery.

Kellogg: Swing away.

Mallory: Ells grabs the kid. Takes him somewhere. Kills him. Buries him.

Kellogg: Swing again.

Mallory: Ells grabs the kid, stashes him, I kill Ells, and the kid, God spare him, without food or water, dies.

Kellogg: Where would Ells hide the kid?

Mallory: Man, Ells had enough time to drive to West Virginia and back. Or Baltimore and back. Or Richmond and back. Right? Kid could be anywhere.

Kellogg: How about Ells having a partner?

Mallory: Nah. His last months were traced back fairly well. He had a pickup truck. Florida tags, registered in a cousin's name. Finally found it parked by a Maryland Metro stop, so we figure he took the Metro in when he came down for the kills, or for the return. Nothing interesting in the truck.

Kellogg: Why Henry James?

Mallory: I got a theory about that.

Kellogg: Tell me.

Mallory: The other guys think there's no pattern to Ells's political interests, but I think there is. I think the pattern is that he was fascinated by political extremism. Like, he's desperate to find something to focus his life on. And who was making announcements about the need for interracial harmony in the aftermath of the Simpson verdict? Henry James. Who was getting blasted by liberals and conservatives, blacks and whites, New Africa and LTC, Democrats and Republicans? Henry James. *Everybody* hated Henry

James. And the conversation the black guy told us about, with Ells, got started when they were watching some talk show about interracial couples. And the Jameses were the city's most prominent interracial couple. Like I said, people on all sides hated the Jameses.

Kellogg: That's a strong word.

Mallory: Hate? You should have read the Jameses' mail. I saw some of it. Henry James had a file full of hate mail. Everything from "Die, nigger, die" to "I hope your white masters lynch your sorry Uncle Tom ass, you devil-worshiping new slave-bitch." Wild stuff, from blacks and whites both. Anyway, I think Ells fixated on James during the Simpson trial because he was doing so much television commentary. He saw James as the ultimate target, kind of a make-both-sides-proud target, and went for it. Beyond that I don't want to speculate, because there's nothing more wasteful than trying to attribute rational motives to the mind of a loser piece of shit like Ells. And as far as the boy goes, you got to forget him. Believe me, Kevin, I still care. About the children, I care. But the kid has to be dead. There's no explanation. Even if there was a partner or a group behind Ells, why *wouldn't* they kill the boy, and right away? And there isn't any partner or group. Ells was a sick motherfucker, and sick motherfuckers get rejected even by radical organizations. Sick motherfuckers do sick shit, but they do it alone.

Kellogg nods. Downs his last sip of whiskey as Mallory finishes his beer.

Mallory: You got my address in West Virginia?

Kellogg: Somewhere.

Mallory: Come on out, man. Surrender. Let's face it—

they won. Let's just go hide in those beautiful hills, fish and drink and forget about what this country could have been.

Kellogg: I'm too fat to run.

Mallory: What's here for you?

Kellogg: Ain't nothing for me anywhere, John.

At an auditorium a few blocks away, Khalid is onstage. He is an actor. He loves the spotlight, the attention, the followers.

As he is introduced, the crowd roars with approval. He raises his hands—they roar louder.

Hear us, Lord, for we are your divine race.

(The audience quiets, listening.)

The white man, he hates us. He hates us and he fears us, because he knows in his heart that we are his superior. He can see what we can all see, that when the playing field is level, we dominate. If we were free to compete on a equal basis in medicine and engineering and law, we would dominate those fields as we dominate the playing fields. And the whites know this to be true, so they deny us that level playing field.

My people, you know what I am going to say, because you have been here before, as we have always been here, and what I say is the truth, but I am going to say it again and again and again until we are *free.*

(Applause, shouts, amens.)

The *only* way we will ever be free is to have our own country, our own land, our own courts, our own schools, our own, our own, our own.

New Africa is my dream.

(Amen.)

New Africa is my dream.

(Amen.)

But the day is coming when it will be our reality. And I tell you that the way to freedom is to use white people's hate and fear against them. We chased them out of the cities by using their fear—now we must do the same thing in Georgia and South Carolina. If we have to, we riot. If we have to, we disrupt the schools. If we have to, we attack the white on the street. We turn our angry young men in their organized street gangs into an army of freedom fighters. *Rise*, my young brothers. (The audience's front rows, young black men in hooded sweatshirts, stand. The crowd behind them screams its delight. The young men pump their fists in joy.) The whites fear our crime? Let us use the criminality which they have forced upon us against them. The white has made us into muggers, murderers, robbers, and rapists? Let us mug, murder, rob, and rape *them*. Let us do unto them as they have done unto us. Let us *stop* hurting our own and *start* hurting those who cause our anger. And when their storm trooper police catch our young soldiers, let us sit in the jury box and *set ourselves free*!

(A tremendous roar erupts.)

Let us use the whites' system against *them*.

Let us use the guns they send into our neighborhood against *them*.

Let us use the injustice system they have created against *them*.

Let us use their fear against *them*.

(Khalid mops his sweat-covered face with a handkerchief. Struts about the stage, eyebrows furrowed in fierce concentration.)

Remember the Plan, people.

First: Direct our anger against our enemies, not ourselves.

Second: Have every single defendant demand a jury trial. This will break the injustice system's back.

Third: Make sure that at least one black—and when I say black, I mean true black, not those Uncle Toms who want to "get along"—make sure at least one right-thinking New African is on every jury and votes for acquittal. Period. Acquittal. Every time.

Four: By the time they get a few years of this, believe me, my people, they will *pay* us to leave. They will *gladly* give us a homeland. And then, my people, my beautiful, gracious people, then, and *only* then, will we be able to *truly* sing, "Free at last, free at last, thank God Almighty, *free at last!*"

(Applause, shouts, amens.)

My people, *they* say we can't make it.

(Scattered boos.)

They say we are too *stupid* and *lazy* to make it.

(More boos.)

They say that blacks can't manage things, can't run things, can't organize things

(Boos.)

They say . . .

Long is waiting when Khalid finishes his speech at the rally. He controls his anger.

Long: What about my idea for calling the people out to search for the missing boy?

Khalid: We talked it over and decided it wasn't practical

Plus, Henry James was such a hated man in our community. We didn't think the people would go for it.

Long knows better than to show his anger to Khalid. In prison, when a man betrays you, you smile to his face.

Long: Yeah, I guess you're right. It was just an idea.

Khalid: And it wasn't a bad one. It was a close decision, really.

Long calls his mother. He doesn't know what he can tell her now.

19

"I THINK SHE WANTS ME TO KILL HER," he says.

"Joan Price does? Oh, my God, why?" Passer asks.

She's sitting with the tall, blond man who sometimes serves as Joan Price's bodyguard. He had followed Kellogg's suggestion and called her, though he'd had to wait a day to get his courage up. They're drinking beer at a country bar in a Maryland suburb. Passer drove out early to trade her car for Desormeaux's truck, to keep up appearances in her role as Adelia Desormeaux. She and the bodyguard have been talking for an hour now.

"Well," he says, "it's this theory she has about the power of victimization. Don't ask me to get it right, because I don't really understand it. But it's something like, because we live in a time of television imagery, that whoever gets to show themselves suffering the most gets the most sympathy. And after you establish yourself as a victim, you can attack as much as you want."

Passer's on her second beer. Listening to the soft, pretty music. Looking at the bodyguard and seeing that he's actually attractive, with his bright-blue eyes, slender build, tight jeans, sweet smile. He's her age but seems younger. Less traveled, although he served in Kuwait and saw action there. He'd enlisted in the army right out of high school, and served four years, and now was out, going to the University of Maryland but unable to feel comfortable there, he said, for political reasons.

"Liberals always talk about inclusion," he said, "but you ought to try going to college these days as a Christian white. The blacks there, man, we're supposed to need them so the place will be more integrated, but they have their own paper, own section of the dining hall, own academic department, own frats, own student government. They're even building a black-only student union so they won't have to see us between classes. When I was in the army, we all worked together and bunked together and ate together. That was cool. But at Maryland, man, it's like, the blacks hate us so much they want everything separate from us, you know?"

"But would you really want to go to an all-white school?" Passer asked, slipping out of character, maybe because of the beer.

"No, that isn't what I said. Just the opposite. But in the army, the blacks carried their weight and didn't have to worry about respect. At Maryland, though, you can tell, they're struggling. Nah, it ain't blacks I hate at all; it's the goddamned government."

"Yeah. Me, too."

"You know? They're such liars."

"Yeah, like Ruby Ridge, and Waco."

"Yeah! Waco, man, letting the FBI handle the investigation—that don't make no sense. You can't let an accused criminal handle his own investigation. 'Excuse me, sir, we think you may have raped this woman, would you please investigate yourself and tell us if you did?'"

"You ever feel like doing something like that guy did in Oklahoma City?"

"Ahh." The boy drank from his beer. Looked at Passer. He had trouble looking her in the eye, intoxicated by more than just the alcohol. "You know, I went downtown once, to Fifteenth and L, because I was so mad about what one of those black racist writers at the *Post* wrote that I felt like blowing up the building. I'm just so sick of the bullshit hate that paper puts out, I really thought about giving them a taste of their own medicine."

"What changed your mind?"

"You know, I don't want to hurt no one. It's kind of a daydream sometimes, but I couldn't really do it. I just get so angry, that's all."

He took a drink. "But when I saw those victims at Oklahoma City, especially the children, man, it scared me. I mean, I've been angry enough to bomb. I couldn't, but still I can understand it, you know? It's just such a bullshit world."

A few minutes later, he makes that statement about Joan Price wanting him to kill her.

"Do you think she was serious?" Passer asks.

"I think so. She wanted me to kill her downtown, while she was driving through some black neighborhood, so the blacks would be blamed."

"She would do that? Go that far for the cause?"

"Joan's serious about stuff."

"I know. I hope she is. But I can't believe she'd really want you to kill her."

"She's serious about everything. She said, once, she thought about suicide every day."

"Really?"

"She said it just all gets to her, that no one can get along, that there's no future, no hope for our species."

"I feel that way sometimes," Passer says sincerely.

Passer asks about Ells. The bodyguard says he never heard of him before the murders. She asks if LTC has anything more "direct" going on, because she really is willing to do anything to help the cause. He says they just do political stuff.

She leaves the young man in the parking lot. He tries to kiss her good night, but she turns her cheek. He doesn't press. She tells him to drive carefully. He tells her the same thing.

She drives out to Frederick, to trade the truck back for her car. Desormeaux is awake when she pulls up at his house. He comes out and tells her that the answering machine has a message for "Adelia." She goes in. Listens. It's Joan Price, asking her to call tonight.

Passer calls. Joan asks her to come over, gives directions. Passer drives there in the pickup truck, hoping maybe she's going to be included in something big but bothered by Joan's tone of voice. It seemed too upbeat. Deliberately upbeat. Passer has good instincts about little changes in people's behavior. From Kellogg, she's learned the importance of trusting those instincts.

✳

Joan Price drives to the nearest twenty-four-hour convenience store. Buys milk and eggs and bacon (having first made sure there were none already in her refrigerator—she had poured out half a bottle of milk to do that). Tries to pay for the purchase with a hundred-dollar bill, which the clerk at this hour (midnight) of course cannot break. Pays for it with some ones and loose change instead. She chats a minute with the clerk, expressing concern about whether it might rain tomorrow, as it did earlier today.

This convenience store is on a major commercial strip in Prince George's County and is surrounded by racially mixed neighborhoods. But the crime here is not so mixed. The store has been robbed six times in the past year, always by blacks. There have been four assaults in the store parking lot in that time, all by blacks.

The store adjoins a divided highway from which there is no left turn out of the parking lot. Customers needing to turn left, as Joan does to get home, go around the back of the store, down the alley there, to a side street. Joan pulls through this alley. There is a shopping center's unwindowed rear wall on one side of the alley, and the convenience store's unwindowed rear wall on the other. No homes. No traffic now.

Joan pulls up at the stop sign there, looks around, sees no one, and dashes to a sewer drain. She crushes the hundred-dollar bill into a ball, lights it with a match, burns it down, brushes the ashes into the drain, hearing the water rushing there from the earlier rain (which is good, she thinks, because she knows homicide investigators might check the drain).

She returns to her car and reaches into the back seat,

where she has a large, helium-filled balloon held down by a heavy blanket. She holds it out the driver's-side window (the night is warm enough to warrant the window's being rolled down).

She's tied a thick cloth napkin to the bottom of the balloon (having tested the balloon before to make sure it could carry the napkin away).

She dumps her now moneyless purse's contents out the driver's-side window and drops the purse itself after it. She gets her gun, the same one she used to kill the drug dealer downtown, from the glove compartment.

She grips the gun in her left hand, by the open driver's-side window (she's right-handed).

She's already wiped the gun free of all prints.

She holds the gun with the napkin, very lightly, using only her thumb and forefinger. She looks straight down the barrel, down that dark tunnel. As she has at least once a day since she lost her family, and every night after every speech, overwhelmed always by the futility of it all, the unfairness she knows is in her words, unable to stop what she's doing in any other way. She's so tired. But even with this, her last mortal act, she's determined to accomplish something.

She prays. Pulls the trigger.

People who are planning to kill themselves don't buy groceries first.

They don't make plans to meet someone later that night.

They don't use their left hand when they're right-handed.

They don't express concern for the next day's weather in small talk with convenience-store clerks.

Their hands don't pass gunpowder-residue tests.

They aren't missing a hundred dollars (which the clerk saw she had).

They don't do it at a side street's stop sign.

They usually leave a note.

Women almost never use a gun.

No one shoots themselves in the eye.

And suburban whites don't use guns whose slugs later match up with unsolved D.C. drug dealer homicides.

As Joan well knows. Just as she knows that even if her plan isn't perfect, there will be enough evidence contradicting a ruling of suicide to satisfy those wanting to believe she was murdered. By someone certainly assumed to be a black.

Passer finds a note on Joan's door, saying: "Adelia, I've gone to the store. Back in a sec. Let yourself in, make yourself comfortable. Joan."

The police come by just then and, after some questions, tell Passer that her friend has been murdered.

Passer starts trembling. She has trouble breathing. After what she learned from the bodyguard, she can't believe Joan was murdered, but she can't believe it was suicide, either.

She sits down on the steps.

She remembers going to a movie once on a date with a black man, to a theater in a black neighborhood, to see a film made by a black director, with black actors, for black people.

The theater that night was packed, all black. The movie's opening scene was of two black males going into a store, robbing it, and killing the Asian storekeeper. And as the storekeeper's head exploded from the black male's gunshot, as Passer cringed at the sight, she heard a roar around her and was stunned by the more horrible sight, not on the screen but in the audience, of people laughing, clapping, cheering, high-fiving. All around her. Everyone. Her date too. She cried. Her date didn't understand. She left. He wrote her off as weird.

She remembers hearing a famous writer, a black woman, say she was surprised to still be alive, because as a young woman she'd been sure she'd kill herself, so constantly depressed about the world was she. Passer understood that.

She remembers that while working as a youth on one of black mayor Tom Bradley's campaigns in Los Angeles, she heard about a black woman columnist in Chicago who'd written an essay, during a racially divisive election, about why she hated whites. Passer had looked up that essay. Read it. Understood the hurt, anger, and *exhaustion* behind it. Researched further and found that the columnist had later killed herself. Understood that too.

Sitting on the front steps at Joan Price's house, sheltered from the drizzle by a slight overhang, late at night in a silent suburb, she sees, across the street, a balloon drifting slowly along the treetops, something hanging from it, she can't tell what.

20

LONG IS AT HIS MOTHER'S HOUSE, in her kitchen. The phone rings. His mother answers. Looks confused. Looks at Long.

"It's for you," she says, stunned.

Long and his mother stare at each other, not understanding how someone would know to call him here.

"Is it that white man, Kellogg, or that girl, Passer?"

"It's a black man."

He takes the phone. Listens a moment to the silence.

"Anybody there?" says a familiar voice. "Long?"

Long: Yeah.

Khalid: Know who this is?

Long: Yeah.

Silence.

Khalid, dejected: Then I guess it's true.

Long: What?

Khalid: I can't believe it. I had to call to be sure.

Long: What?

Khalid: You're Henry James's brother.

Long: Yeah, that's right. Who gives a fuck?

Khalid laughs. Sadly: Man, I'm sorry.

Long, keeping his echoing, deep, emotionless voice: What's up? How'd you know I'm here?

Khalid: That's the same thing as asking how I know you're Henry James's brother, isn't it?

Long: How you know?

Khalid: It don't matter.

Long: How you know?

Khalid: Listen, man. The boy is dead.

Long is silent.

Khalid: I mean, he will be soon. Real soon. Good as dead.

Long: What's going on?

Khalid: I can't tell you. I'm sorry. It's not my people doing it. It's not my people who found him.

Long's anger is rising: Where is he, Khalid? What's going on?

Khalid: The boy called your house a little while ago. Talked to his sister for a minute, to tell her he'd be home tomorrow. The number he called from led back to a pay phone across the street from where he was.

Long: Led back? By who?

Khalid: The people who are probably still listening.

Long: Who?

Khalid: The boy's your nephew? I'm sorry, brother. It's just the way it goes.

Long: Where's the boy, Khalid?

Khalid: Look, man. It's like this. Those stupid FBI

motherfuckers the Director put in charge of city corruption investigation? I told you about that little arrangement. The Goof Squad. Well, they also are handling the tap on your mother's phone, 'cause the Director wanted to know all that's going on with the videotapes shit.

Long: Tell me where the boy is, Khalid. That's all you got to do.

Khalid: You got to forget him, Long. He's gone, okay? I mean, he saw too much. He knows too much. Okay?

Long: He's just a boy, Khalid.

Khalid: Shit, man, I ain't happy about it! But like you said when you gave that order that time in the joint—about how I had to take out that homeboy of mine who weren't nothing but eighteen—death ain't no thing.

Long, forcing calm into his voice: Khalid, give me the boy.

Mrs. James has been listening closely.

Khalid: Long, it's out of my hands. He does know too much. And I don't just mean all the videotapes he saw. I mean, he saw someone knifed tonight.

Long: Who?

Khalid: The man who found him and took him in, the night of the murders. The man who's been hiding him all this time.

Long: Who's that?

Khalid: Come on, man. Just let it go. The boy is gone. Good as gone. They're just interrogating him a little more now, 'cause they're scared he might have called someone else besides his sister. They want to know who else might know what he knows. But I left there ten minutes ago. They probably done the boy by now.

Long: Khalid, listen now. You owe me, right? Tell me that. Tell me you owe me.

Khalid: I owe you.

Long: Then tell me where the boy is.

Silence.

Long: Come on, man.

Click.

"God damn it!" Long yells, banging the phone against the wall.

His mother looks at him. "They found the boy? But what? What else?"

Long can't answer. He looks into his mother's terror-filled eyes and can't answer.

He moves quickly to the stairwell landing, bounds up the steps four at a time. Opens his niece's door without knocking.

She's on her bed, watching television. Looks up at him as he bursts in.

"Girl, where's your brother?"

She looks at Long, frightened.

He realizes that and softens his features, his voice. "Girl, I need to know where he is."

"I don't know. I *don't!*"

"Did he say anything about where he was? Like, what neighborhood?"

"No."

"Did he say if he was in a house or an apartment?"

"He said he was in a basement."

"Good, good. Now, when did he call you?"

She thinks about what was on television when he called,

looks at her clock, figures it out. "An hour and ten minutes ago."

"Yes," Mrs. James says. "I remember the phone rang, but it's almost always one of her girlfriends, so I let her get it."

The girl speaks quickly. "He said not to tell you! He asked me if anything happened when his letter came, and I said no, and he said nobody did anything, no police did anything, or FBI? And I said no, and he said then maybe it *was* safe to come home, and I said I thought so because Uncle Long was here, and he said I was lying, and I said no I am *not*, and Uncle Long is so big *nobody* can hurt us now, and he said Uncle Long is really there? and I said yes! and he said maybe it really *was* safe to come home, and I said, should I get Grandma? and he said no, because she'll want him to come home now, and she'll tell the police and the FBI and he wouldn't be able to convince her not to except by showing her the videotapes he had, that Daddy had, that explained why it might be the police or FBI that *killed* Mommy and Daddy." She started to cry. "I knew I should have told you, Grandmommy."

"That's okay, hon," Long says. "That's okay. Now who did he say he was with?"

"A man."

"Okay. Who?"

"I don't know."

"You don't know the man, or he didn't tell you?"

"He said it was a man I didn't know."

"Did *he* know him?"

"No, the man found him. In the alley that night, behind our house."

"What kind of man?"

"I don't know."

"Black or white?"

"I don't know."

He spends a few minutes asking the girl more questions, but she can't tell him anything else. His mother sits with the girl. Long goes downstairs.

He goes out the back door, through the little yard there, to the alley. Thinks, who might have been in a city alley at night? Thinks, the police would have asked everyone who was around that night, that morning. Even the reporters would have. But what about whoever wasn't around any-more?

He sets out at a run for his brother's house. Goes to the alley behind the house. Looks around. Sees no one. Goes down a block, sees no one. Back up a block, sees no one. Crosses the street. Down the street, sees a couple of black men passing a bottle in a brown paper bag, drinking from it. He goes to them.

Long has spent too much time on the street and in the joint not to know how to handle such men as these.

"Hey," he says, coming up to them.

They eye his gaunt figure and stern eyes. Nod.

In a deep, serious voice, he asks, "You going to tell me something?"

One of the men drawls out, "Shit," and Long grabs the man by the throat, stares ferociously down into his eyes.

That man, and the other, have spent too much time on the street and in jail themselves not to know that a man such as the one confronting them now will do what he needs to get what he needs.

"What's up?" asks the other man.

"I need some information," Long says.

"That ain't hard," says the man whose neck Long is letting go.

"I want y'all to tell me who you ain't seen for a while. I mean, out here. Who hanging out here, round here, you ain't seen for about a week."

"Man, that's some people, you know," says the second man. "But now, don't get mad, let me think. You mean, like the white folk living here? You wanting to know who's on vacation so you can take their house down?"

"I'm talking about the brothers that hang here."

The two men think. Look at each other. The first man, the one Long grabbed, says, "Ain't seen Preacher for a while."

"How long a while?" Long asks.

"Like you say, about a week."

"He hang around here?"

"Here. Downtown some. He ain't checking in, though, you know."

"I know. What's his thing? Wine?"

"Oh, wine, sure. Whatever. He's a case. Upstairs."

Long takes that to mean he has some mental illness. "But is he together?"

"Yeah, he stays together well enough."

"Violent?"

"No, no. Not Preacher."

"You know him to sleep in that alley back there?"

"He's got that one doorway staked out. Back door to the Thai place. Stays there when it rains. Rest of the time, I think he's got some place he goes to. His grandmother's place. She got some basement in her house I think he stays wintertime. That house might be abandoned now, though, because I think he said she died a few months ago and that old house wasn't worth nothing, out in nowhere."

"Where's that?"

"I don't know. Never been there. He ain't going to bring no one there, 'cause his grandmother didn't even want him there. She was ninety year old and didn't hardly trust him. Sure wasn't going to trust me. She only let him in the basement. Not upstairs. I think that what he told me."

The other man says, "Maybe he just don't want to bring you over."

"Fuck you," the first man says.

"I need to know where it is," Long says.

"Don't know. Northeast, all I know."

"What's his whole name?"

"Oh, man, don't be asking me nobody's whole name!" He points to his companion. "I don't even know this mother-fucker's whole name."

"His name's Bobby Jay," the other man says. "I mean, that's what he says it is, don't he? Preacher Bobby Jay?"

Long gets a description, approximate age. Can't get any other hard information.

Rain has fallen much of the day, and the streets are wet, shining under headlights, glistening under lamps. The warm yellow windows of homes sparkle with tense drops. The air is cool, clean; the sky cloudy, orange-tinted from the under-flow of the city's lights.

Long passes his brother's house. Murder site. Looks at the darkened windows.

He jogs quickly back to his mother's house, a spectral

form in his black jeans, black jacket. The few people on the sidewalks step aside well before they're in his way, if they see him before he's on them.

He tells his mother what he found out, then opens a phone book. Looks for a Jay listed in Northeast.

Finds only one. Calls it.

A young woman answers. Babies are crying in the background. Long asks just a few questions before he's satisfied it's not the house he's looking for. The young woman also claims no knowledge of any elderly female relatives in the city, especially none that died lately. She's never heard of a Preacher Bobby Jay.

Long hangs up. Thinks. Grimacing, calls Kellogg.

Kellogg is in his booth in the diner. He answers on the cellular phone, thinking it's probably Passer. He's surprised it's Long.

Long: Listen, man. I need an address.

Kellogg: Whose?

Long: If I give you the last name of a person who's supposed to own a house, can you find their address?

Kellogg: If it's that simple. If they own the house, not rent. If you got the name right. Sure. Why?

Long has been hesitant to ask for help his whole life, always.

Long: I think I got the last name of a place where the boy might be.

Kellogg inhales sharply.

Long: He's alive.

Kellogg: How do you know?

Long explains. Tells him the name, Bobby Jay. Kellogg shakes his head, feels a rush in his blood.

Kellogg: Call me back from a pay phone in five minutes.

Long leaves the house. Goes to a phone. Calls.

Kellogg: You?

Long: Yeah.

Kellogg: I got it.

Long: Give it up.

Kellogg: I'm coming too.

Long: Ain't your place.

Kellogg: Fuck you.

Long: Shit, motherfucker, what are you good for?

Kellogg: The address.

Long: Shit.

Kellogg: You got a car?

Long is silent.

Kellogg: I'm on the job here.

Long: Is the address in Northeast?

Kellogg: Yeah.

Long: Around CU or the Soldiers Home? Brookland?

Kellogg: No.

Long: Then your white face is going to queer my play.

Kellogg: This ain't a debate, asshole. It's a fact. I'm coming.

Long: All right. Fuck.

Silence.

Long, conceding: We need some more people. Where's your girl Passer?

Kellogg: Working.

Long: Can you get her?

Kellogg: No.

Long: This might be too ugly for her anyway. Shit, man, all the motherfuckers I could trust in a spot this hard are in lockdown. You got anyone you can *really* trust here?

Kellogg: Yeah.

Long: I mean, man, with a gun if it comes to it?

Kellogg: Yeah.

Long: I'm serious, man. This ain't no time for a folder.

Kellogg: Nah, the man I'm thinking of, he won't fold. It's the only man your brother would trust with this. Chavez.

Long, solemnly: Yeah.

Kellogg: He's working, but I know where.

Long: Get him. Fast. I don't know how much time we got, but it might be none. What guns you got?

Kellogg: I don't use guns. Don't you have some?

Long: I'm on parole. You don't have a gun? A redneck motherfucker like you don't have a gun?

Kellogg: I got an old rifle.

Long: Bring it, then. You got fifteen minutes to get here.

Long gives him the street corner he's calling from.

Kellogg: Be there.

Long: I'll be there. I'm going to get me a piece first, but I'll be there.

Kellogg hangs up. Gets moving. Doesn't doubt that Long can find and buy a gun in fifteen minutes.

Kellogg goes to his office. Gets the rifle and bullets from the closet.

He moves as quickly as his body lets him to his fake taxi. Drives as quickly as the streets let him to Georgetown. Blocks the alley when he parks behind the restaurant where Chavez works. Stomps up the steps of the restaurant's back door, opens it without knocking, sees Chavez in dirty white work clothes, scrubbing pots.

Chavez looks up when the back door opens. Sees

Kellogg. Sees the look on his face. Comes instantly when Kellogg silently beckons him out. Without a word, gets in the car with Kellogg. Only when they are moving does he ask, What?

Kellogg tells him.

Long is hidden in an unlit alley across from the corner where Kellogg pulls up for him. He looks things over before stepping out of the dark. Calls out "Yo" as he comes up to Kellogg, so as not to startle the man.

He gets in the back seat. Nods to Chavez when Kellogg makes the introduction.

Kellogg pulls away. Heads across town.

Long: He know what's up? (To Chavez) You know what's up?

Chavez: Yes.

He holds up Kellogg's rifle.

Long: You know how to use that?

Chavez: I know how.

Long: Kellogg, when's the last time you cleaned it?

Kellogg: Never.

Long: Great.

Kellogg: You seem awfully anxious to fight.

Long: I just want the boy.

Kellogg: Me, too.

Chavez: Me, too.

Long: You do know who you're fucking with, don't you? Both of you? The FBI. The police. Maybe New Africa. Seriously backed-up motherfuckers. They can make anything that happens look like anything they want. Especially if no one's around to dispute them.

Kellogg: Don't be so naive.

Long: What? I'm the one telling *you* not to be naive. Cop-trusting white motherfucker like you, you the naive one.

Kellogg: I ain't naive. I'm saying, don't *you* be naive. I mean, they don't have to kill us. Think about who we are: an alcoholic detective run off the police force, a three-time convicted murderer, and a wetback dishwasher.

Long: So I'm saying we go, I make a play to get the boy out. You guys back me up.

Kellogg: You got a play?

Long: You got a phone?

Kellogg hands it to Long, who takes it, dials.

Long: Tell me the address.

Kellogg does.

Khalid, in his office, sweating, answers his phone when it rings.

Long: Hey.

Khalid, who was expecting a call but not from Long: Where are you, man? You ain't doing nothing stupid, are you?

Long tells Khalid the address.

Long: Is that it?

Khalid, sighing: Yeah. How'd you get it?

Long: Don't worry about that.

Khalid: You're not going there, are you?

Long: I'm on my way now.

Khalid, frightened: Listen, brother, you got to think on this. Those men over there, they are scared and stupid, and that's the most dangerous combination there is.

Long: Call them.

Khalid: And tell them what?

Long: Tell them you're sending a man over there to take care of the boy. Tell them it's a stone killer you know will do it right and who, even if he does get caught, will gladly take the rap with his mouth shut because he's such a brainwashed New Africa fuck. They knifed the man who took care of the boy, right? Tell them the guy you're sending over, me, has a prior for knife murder, so he's perfect to take this heat. Tell them they're to give me the knife they used, and the boy, so if I get caught later I'll have the murder weapon on my person. Tell them to let me take the boy away because I've also got a string of molestation charges on my record and one conviction. In fact, tell them you're going to let me take the boy in the woods, do shit to him, kill him, and then they can be hero police and come get me, killing me when I resist arrest. Okay? I know a tall guy just got out of Lorton with this sheet, so if they check their computer the story will fly.

Long gives Khalid that ex-con's name.

Khalid: And what happens when this don't all come through?

Long: You the man, motherfucker. This'll all just give you more shit on the big shots. More control over them.

Khalid: What's going to keep the boy quiet? He saw all the tapes. Saw the homeless man who took him in get cut. How we going to keep him quiet?

Long: I'll keep him quiet. I'll tell him if he talks, he dies. With what he's seen this last week, he knows what death is. I ain't worried about him. He'll be leaving town anyway. I talked with his grandmother, and she's taking him to England, of all the fucking places. Believe me, she's going to back us on this. She's as scared that he'll talk as you are. She wants him alive. She won't let him say boo.

Khalid is quiet.

Long: Do this, man. Come on. I'm the one swimming in the shit. You just get me in the door.

Khalid, sighing: Okay.

Long: I'm on my way, so call them now.

Khalid: Yeah, okay. Okay, man. That is, if they ain't done the boy yet.

Long: Call them *now*. Right?

Khalid: You just play your end right. I'll take care of my part.

Long turns the phone off.

Khalid dials a number for the cellular phone the men at the house are using. A man answers with a grunted uh-huh.

Khalid: Mallory?

Mallory: Yeah.

Khalid: I got a problem and a solution at the same time.

Mallory: What?

Khalid: The boy say anything new?

Mallory: We haven't gotten to him yet. We're still working on this Preacher guy. I should say the FBI agents are working on him. He told them the boy didn't call anyone except his sister. I believe him. He said the boy was in shock the night his parents got killed, and he found him wandering down the alley, and the boy wouldn't let him take him home or to a hospital or the police because he was too scared. I told you all this.

Khalid: This Preacher guy, he saw the tapes, though? He admit that?

Mallory: Yeah. Not at first, but eventually, because he had to explain why he didn't call the police or the FBI, and it's only seeing the tapes that would scare him off doing that.

Khalid: He's still alive? The Preacher guy?

Mallory: I told you, we need him alive when we shoot him, because an autopsy can determine if the shots were postmortem.

Khalid: We can cover that if we need to.

Mallory: Of course. But the fewer people in on this shit the better. Bad enough I got to deal with these Goof Squad idiots. They're scared shitless about getting caught.

Khalid: Aren't you?

Mallory, laughing: I got the tapes, dickwad.

Khalid: Your boss, the Mayor, is going to want them.

Mallory: For a cool million, they're his.

Khalid: I'll give you a million.

Mallory: I knew you didn't make copies!

Khalid realizes he's blown his earlier bluff on that point. Realizes again how incredibly stupid he was not to have made copies.

Khalid: I'll give you a million and a better ticket out of all this. 'Cause you got trouble coming.

Mallory: You said that before.

Khalid: Henry James's brother, Long, got the address somehow. He's on his way over right now. He is the meanest motherfucker you're ever going to meet in your life, and that's his nephew you got there.

Mallory, anger jumping into his voice: You cocksucker, you told him!

Khalid: No.

Mallory: Bullshit! How else could he find out?

Khalid: I don't know. He's smart. Anyway, he's on his way over. Now, *if* you agree to sell *me* the tapes, I won't call him back and tell him I've warned you he's coming. *If* we got a deal, I'll make everything come out right.

Mallory: You cocksucker, you gave him the address to get leverage on me, to make me make this deal.

Khalid: Sounds like something *you'd* do.

Mallory, angrily conceding: All right. What's up?

Khalid: He expects me to tell you to let him take the boy. You're supposed to trust him to finish the boy off and take any rap there might be for Preacher's death too. So that plays into us. When he gets there you tell him Preacher's not dead and that he has to finish him off, so that it really will be him who killed the man.

Mallory: Can this guy Long, can he kill someone with a knife? That ain't the same thing as shooting them.

Khalid: He won't have no trouble with that part. He'll be happy to, to prove his story to you. So you let him in. Let him finish Preacher off. Let him go in the room where you got the boy. Let him get the boy. He's holding a knife in his hand. He's a bloody mess from the first killing. You see him. Shoot him. Then kill the boy, with the knife, and say that Long killed Preacher and the boy, and you killed him.

Mallory: I told you before, I'm not killing the boy. It's hard enough for me to let it happen. I'm sure not doing it myself, and I'm *sure* not doing it with a knife. I told you, there's this one FBI fuck here who's anxious to do it. What a sick fuck. A genuine bigot, if you know what I mean.

Khalid: And you thought they didn't exist anymore.

Mallory: No, I just thought they were all black now.

Khalid: Fine. I don't care. Let him do it. Just make sure

the Preacher and the boy *and* Long get set up the right way. And bring me the tapes. I got your money right here.

Mallory: And I'm not shooting Long. It would be too conspicuous. I'm going to let the FBI handle the whole thing, and I'll just be around to supervise things for the Mayor. The FBI guys, they got their story together without me in the picture. They say they got the address from the wiretap on the grandmother's house. Came over. All the killing started when they knocked on the door and the kidnapper panicked and they had to shoot him, but it was too late to save the boy. Now I guess they'll say Long got here when they did, saw what the Preacher did to the boy, and went crazy stabbing him, and they had to shoot *him*. No, even better—Long, *he* kidnapped the boy, killed the Preacher when he came around, and killed the boy when the FBI showed up, and then they killed him.

He pauses.

Mallory: Man, call Long back and tell him not to come.

Khalid: It's too late.

Mallory: Do you have any idea what a house of cards this all is? What if someone saw us all come in when we did and later testifies as to the discrepancy with our reported time of arrival? That's just one thing. There's so many things that can go wrong. The last thing we need is a new factor. This is all too tender, man. It's too tender to be fucking with.

Khalid: It's too late. Deal with it. With him.

Mallory laughs nervously. Turns off his phone. Shakes his head. He knows the realities. Knows how many fires he'll be putting out and how little chance he has of keeping it together. Thinks about running but knows he has no chance if he does that.

He wonders how he could have let himself get pulled into all this. Just a few hours ago he was home watching television. His phone rang.

It was the Mayor, who told him the FBI director had just called to say the Goof Squad he'd put on the James boy's "kidnapping"—whose sole effort consisted of monitoring the boy's grandmother's house for a ransom call that no one expected would ever come—had got an address for the boy. The Mayor wanted Mallory to go along as his personal representative and liaison. Specifically, to get the tapes. Of all the Mayor's police, Mallory was the one he turned to when he needed someone to work with white cops or, in this case, FBI agents, because Mallory was the only white cop in the Mayor's police club.

So Mallory went with the Goof Squad to get the kid. To get the tapes (although the Director was to be allowed New Africa's blackmail tape of him). But not to hurt the kid. To be part of the rescue team.

Then the man who'd found the boy that night, Preacher—who had not known who the boy was or why he was wandering around the alley, but had just taken him to his own emergency home and nursed him, as he could better than almost anyone because he'd been through so much himself—then that man, upon answering the door tonight, turned to run out the back. Mallory was the one knocking on the door. The agents were in the back. They pushed Preacher back inside.

Preacher, strangely terrified, maybe from having seen the tapes, from thinking the Jameses were killed for them, grabbed a kitchen knife. Came at one of the agents. The agent ducked aside, grabbed the man's knife hand. Another agent, the psycho bigot, grabbed the knife and, furiously, started cutting Preacher. Mallory stepped in, but it was too late. Preacher was cut too bad to live long without emergency medical treatment, and maybe not even then. And the agents said they weren't going to let one of their own go before a black jury on murder charges. These agents were the biggest fools the Director could pull together, and now their stupidity was blowing up on them all. They refused to call for local police or an ambulance.

The agents called the Director, who told them to set up the frame on the Preacher. (Mallory called the Mayor, who, upon hearing what had happened, said the line was bad and hung up.)

The agents locked the boy in a closet until they could decide if it was necessary to kill him. Mallory searched for and found the videos, while the agents interrogated the dying man, who, they learned, called himself Preacher.

Although the home was owned by Preacher's grandmother, and she was dead, the estate had not been settled. The electricity was still on, and there was a VCR and a television.

Mallory, using the VCR, fast-forwarded through the tapes, none of which were very long, to make sure of what he had. He'd seen them all before, of course. Except for one.

It was of Henry and Jessica James, and Jimmy Close, of all people. Mallory, curious as to whether the tape might have some of the same value as the others, watched a minute.

Jimmy Close: I have this woman now, Joan Price, she's a tiger. Electric. The best public speaker I've ever seen in person. But her push is Nazi-like to me somehow. That's not fair, I know, and we all use the Hitler allegation too easily, but still I can't help but see how quick she is to say "they" hate "us" and then use that as justification to hate back. She's not the only one that does it. She's just better at it than most. And white. She's got this thing now where all she does to warm up an audience before she speaks is set up a big-screen TV and play tapes of blacks cheering the Simpson verdict. She lets that picture of the smug face of racial victory sink in to the white audience. Has a banner hanging over the screen saying "Eighty percent of blacks think Simpson is innocent of a crime because eighty percent of blacks don't think that killing whites is a crime."

Henry James: Every bigot in America, black and white, loved that verdict.

Mallory fast-forwarded to check for anything important. He stopped to listen one more moment and heard Henry James say: "I know what you mean. I've got a brother, an older brother, named Long. He's well known in this city, on the streets. The city doesn't know he's my brother and would hardly believe it. But I know it, and I never forget it. Not a day goes by I don't think about how he lost his own life's value so many years ago. It's his fault, not society's. It happens to whites as well as blacks. But all those people we're losing, we have to find. That's what my life is about. I think that's what yours is too, brother."

James put his hand out to Jimmy Close. They shook.

The agents came out of the kitchen. They said Preacher claimed the boy didn't know anything. They said the man would die soon. What should they do? They asked Mallory if he could clear this with the homicide dicks. The agents had a plan to kill the kid and then frame Preacher for it. They'd use what they had on the Mayor (the white-hooker blow-job tape) and on the police chief (the black cop shooting the handcuffed Latino) if they had to. But they wanted protection here. Was he in?

Mallory knew the story was bound to spring a leak, but he'd sail it as far as it went. In the meantime, he needed money. Insurance money. Get-the-fuck-out-of-here money. And of all the powerful people he knew, the one with the most money right now, the one with the most to gain from having all the tapes, the one most able to scheme and manipulate with those tapes, the smartest one, was Khalid.

Mallory called Khalid. Said, Come over. Now. You're only a couple of minutes away, and I got the tapes. He didn't tell Khalid about the boy or Preacher, only about the tapes.

Khalid came, and merely by walking in the place he got himself in trouble. He left as quickly as he could, after briefly viewing the tapes to make sure they were the real thing. After seeing the Henry James–Jimmy Close tape. After hearing the stunning (to him) revelation that Long Ray was Henry James's brother.

"That guy Long works with me," Khalid said to Mallory. "And he's Henry James's brother? Wow. No wonder he's been so interested in finding this boy."

"I know that name," Mallory said. "Long Ray. He's done time? Murder?"

Khalid nodded.

"What a chain of events Ells started that night," Mallory said.

Kellogg, disgusted by Long's talk with Khalid, says, as he drives them across town: You really are an idiot.

Long: It's my ass.

Kellogg: Mine, too.

Long: Let's just get there and see what it looks like. I came up with this 'cause what else we going to do—shoot our way in? Call the cops or the FBI?

They drive a minute in silence. Through a city they all know well—and differently.

They come to the street. Warehouses, abandoned homes, vacant lots, closed corner stores. It's ten at night. The streets are quiet.

Kellogg parks around the corner from the house.

Long: Listen, man, you're just going to pull up like a regular cabbie. There's still a couple of white cabbies in this town, and they're all fat like you. You pull up in front, let me out, and wait for me, like I'm just your fare. Chavez, you duck down.

Kellogg: They probably got someone on the porch. Someone else checking the back window. They're probably all checking out all the windows. Arcides, how about we drop you off up the block. You take the rifle. If there's a problem, Long is likely to come barreling out with those mother-fuckers right behind. I'll keep the engine running. You just be ready to give us a couple of covering shots. This is if Long comes out at all.

Long: If I don't?

Kellogg: If they buy me as a cabbie, then I guess they'll come out and give me some story about how you're staying, and pay me the fare and send me on my way. If they recognize me—and since they're cops and FBI they might have seen me sometime—then we're fucked anyway.

Long takes his ball cap off, gives it to Kellogg.

Long: Wear this down low. Stay in the car. Park so the streetlight's angle puts a shadow on your face.

Kellogg nods.

Kellogg: If they do send me off, I'm going to assume your plan is cooked.

Long: Which leaves you doing what?

Kellogg: Calling 911. Calling the fire department. Calling the *Post* and the FBI, even. Calling everyone. The more of a circus we can make, the harder it'll be for these guys to pull off whatever story they've concocted to explain the bodies. They got pull up high, so they can probably pull off a frame. But I don't think that shit's ever as easy as the movies make out. I guarantee you, every guy in there is waiting for the bottom to fall out of all this. They know law enforcement, which means they know how good a chance there is that someone will talk if confronted, to save his own ass. They know the first one to talk gets the deal. On the other hand, these guys, they probably got a plan for dealing with a call to the police. They know there's some chance of a neighbor or passerby hearing something, a scream maybe, and calling in. If I were them, I'd have a squad car they can trust waiting nearby, so it can take the call and be first on the scene and handle it right. Still, if it's all we can do, it's all we can do.

Long: If they come out and tell you I don't need a cab anymore, tell them you heard a shout. If nothing else, I'll try to scream, like you say, so a neighbor, or you, the cabbie, have an excuse to call it in. But don't leave. I ain't asking you this for me. I'm saying for the boy. Be persistent. Honk the horn. Wake up the neighborhood. Make those calls.

Chavez: I will come running too, like I heard a noise too. I will say, What is happening? And refuse to leave.

Kellogg: That'll make it harder for them to explain what they were doing here before any call came in. I'll bet they're going to have someone call in reporting the murder, so they can come out and investigate it themselves and make sure it all gets handled right. They got to have some plan. But they might have a lot of plans. Contingency plans. Shit, all they got to do is say they got tipped, came over, found the boy dead, and killed the wino, Preacher. They kill the boy with the wino's knife. Claim the wino started stabbing himself—I've seen it happen—and when they tried to stop him he came at them and they had to shoot him. They'll put a few bullets into his body to back the story up. Then it's just a few forensic realities to fix, and they're home free. The FBI's presence can be explained because they're part of the team investigating the boy's disappearance. They can even say they're the ones who got the tip and brought Metro in for the arrest. See? That's a story I just made on the spot. These guys have had time. They'll have figured out the angles. We got to throw a monkey wrench into it.

He looks at Long.

Long: Don't be calling me no monkey.

Kellogg: Pull off your play, man.

Chavez: Come on. The boy is in danger.

Kellogg: Get out here, Arcides. Go down this alley and up the side street. Stay out of sight. Come as far down the front of the block as you can, but don't let anyone see you. Even in this city, a man walking around with a rifle's going to get attention. And if there is a squad car nearby, look out for them. Look out for other lookouts, for that matter.

Chavez nods. Gets out. Looks around carefully. Trots quickly off.

Kellogg: Ready?

Long: Do it.

Kellogg: Your gun is a waste. They'll take it from you first thing.

Long: Fuck 'em.

Kellogg drives to the house. Double-parks in front. Sees a curtain pull back, peeking width.

Long inhales. Gets out. Stretches. Cool. Walks up the sidewalk path, through the weedy, scruffy lawn to the peeling wood porch. Up the steps. An unshaded bulb over the door lights his face.

He knocks. A barely audible voice tells him to come in. He does.

Mallory closes the door behind Long. Puts a gun to his ear.

Mallory: You don't mind if we frisk you, do you?

Long lifts his shirt, revealing the gun stuck inside his pants. Mallory takes it.

Mallory: Still got to frisk you. You understand.

Long: Sure.

Mallory: We got a delicate situation here.

Long, as one of the agents searches him, says: I know. Khalid told me.

Long is taking everything in. The furniture. The number of men. The looks on their faces. The white plastic gloves on their hands. Where the doors and windows are.

Mallory: So you're going to take care of things for us.

Long: Khalid told me to.

Mallory leads Long into the kitchen, where Preacher lies unconscious on the floor in a pool of blood.

Mallory: There's the knife. On the counter. Finish the guy off.

Long, without hesitating, takes the knife, kneels beside Preacher, cuts his throat.

He stands. Faces Mallory.

Long: Where's the punk?

Mallory: The boy?

Long: Yeah. The boy.

Mallory, pointing down the hall: There's a big closet back there. No windows. He's in there.

Long: I'm going to take him away. Do him out in the woods.

One of the agents speaks: Nah, do him here. It'll be better.

Long: I do what Khalid tells me to do. Khalid said take him out to the woods and do him there.

Agent, pointing a gun at Long, speaking slowly: Do him here.

Long: Fine. In the closet or the kitchen?

Agent: Who cares? You do him, or I will.

Long: I'll do him. He's the son of that James asshole, who was trying to hurt Khalid? It'll be an honor to kill the little punk. Want me to do him here? Fine. What do I care? But I don't want no witnesses. Especially not white ones.

He is cold. Mean. Heartless. So believable Mallory almost forgets it's an act.

Long strides purposefully down the hall, knife in hand. Aware of doors and windows and men. Aware of who's where in relation to what.

He opens the door of a walk-in closet. Sees the terrified boy huddled in a corner, shaking, eyes wide.

Long, over his shoulder: I'm doing the kid here.

He shuts the door behind him. Kneels down. Speaks in the softest tone of his life: Stay cool, boy. I'm getting you out of here.

The boy doesn't understand. Long, whispering: I'm not going to hurt you. Okay? But we got to move fast. I got to get you out of here.

The boy, his thin voice trembling: Do you have a gun?

Long: No.

Boy: Then how can you get me out? There's five of them, and they have guns.

Long sucks in a deep breath: Boy? I'm going to get you out.

He leans closer. Holds the boy. Feels him struggle. Hears him cry out: No!

Long, fiercely: I'm not going to hurt you!

Boy: Who are you?

Long: I'm your uncle Long.

The boy stares. Then leaps onto Long, grabbing him tightly around the neck.

Long lets out a deeply held breath. Thinks, I need five seconds. There's a window in the room just to the right when I step out of here. A window on the street side. I know these motherfuckers are onto me. I think their play is to just shoot me when I step out this door and fix my ex-con ass for all the shit. I smell that on them. See it in their eyes. But if I can just get five seconds. Three seconds, even. Just so they don't shoot as soon as I open this door. Just so I can duck inside that room and bust out that window.

Long: Boy, there's a man outside in a cab. He's a friend

of your father's, and he's going to drive us out of here. Okay?
We're just making a break for it. Okay?

The boy nods.

Long: If these guys let us walk out, cool. I got a story
going with them, and if they're buying, we're easy out. But if
not, then fuck 'em. We're just busting, okay?

The boy nods.

Long: If we got to, we're just diving out the window and
running fast as we can to the cab. You got it?

The boy nods.

Long: You just think about running. You see that man—
he's a big fat white man—and you run to him. Don't worry
about me. Don't look back. I'll take care of these motherfuckers. Now tell me, what are you going to do?

Boy: Run to the white man in the cab.

Long stands. Hears one of the agents call out: What the
fuck are you doing?

Long thinks of telling the boy to scream. Decides instead to make him scream. He needs a real convincing
scream, and blood. He needs the agents to hear the scream.
They're not expecting him to really hurt the boy, so they'll
be confused if he does. He needs to open the door and have
them be confused at what they're seeing. Have them looking
twice to see what's going on.

He takes the knife. Speaks in an impossibly deep voice:
Be strong, boy. He takes the knife and slashes the boy's arm.
The boy screams. Bleeds. Long slashes him across the belly.
Not deeply at all, but painfully, so the boy's second scream is
as real as the first, and the blood comes out. Long picks the
boy up with one hand, holds the bloody knife in the other.
Tells the boy to play dead.

He opens the closet door. Steps out.

The agents, guns ready, stare at him. They thought he was going to fake killing the boy. Did he really do it? They stare.

Long—a lifetime of death-if-you're-wrong instincts coming through—knows he was right about their plans. They weren't going to let him out.

He moves.

One step out to the door on the right. Two steps across to the window.

He hears a gunshot. Knows he doesn't have time to open the window.

He tucks the boy into his chest and dives headfirst out the window, but he doesn't make it all the way through. He feels his legs catch on the sill as he spills out. Hanging upside down, slashed by broken glass, he drops the boy. Hears another gunshot. Another. Feels one of the agents hit his feet. Long kicks at him. Another agent sticks his gun out the window. Down. At Long. Fires. Twice. In Long's face.

Kellogg, alerted first by muffled screams, starts out of the car when he hears the first shot. A moment later he sees Long come crashing through a window. Sees him caught there. Sees the boy fall out of his arms, hit the ground, bleeding. Hears more gunshots.

He calls to the boy: Run!

The boy does.

Kellogg sees arms with guns poking from the window over Long. Sees Long try to kick up at them. Sees Long get killed. Sees two other men with guns come through the front door, across the porch.

The boy is running, but he won't make it. Kellogg steps

as quickly as he can, more quickly than anyone might have believed, to grab the boy. Meets the boy on the lawn. The men open fire. Kellogg can't get the boy to the car.

All he can do is grab the child and spin him around, sheltering him with his own huge body. He feels a bullet punch in his back. Another. A third. He drops to his knees, holding the boy as tightly as he can.

Arcides Chavez was a hundred yards away when he heard the first shot. He jumped up from where he was hiding behind a hedge. Started running when he heard the glass breaking. Saw, as best he could in the dark, Long coming through the window. Saw the boy fall from Long's arms and start running to Kellogg. Saw the men come out firing their guns. Saw Kellogg grab the boy. Saw Kellogg get hit.

Arcides Chavez has a rifle. He wishes he lived in a world where there were no rifles, but he doesn't. Never did. Not as a child in El Salvador. Not here. But Arcides Chavez doesn't just have the rifle, he has a talent for it. He took his first target shots at six, could hit the targets by eight, was the best marksman in the village at ten, the best in the mountains at twelve, the best, period, at fourteen. But he wasn't there, rifle in hand, when the soldiers killed his father, or the town spy turned in his mother to the government. He wasn't there, rifle in hand, when his wife was raped and killed in the streets of this American city.

He stops. Drops to his knee. With no tears in his eyes or tremble in his hands, he focuses. Aims. Fires.

Twice.

The two men who came out of the house to pull Kellogg's body off the boy shake. Look at each other. See the wounds in each other's chests and figure out what they mean. Drop.

Chavez runs to the boy. Keeps his eyes on the house's windows, gun ready. Grabs the boy and pulls him to the other side of the cab. Hears sirens. Decides to just wait. It's all he can think to do.

From the house he hears yells and gunshots.

21

THE SHOTS FROM THE HOUSE WERE MALLORY'S. He'd realized, as the two agents dropped from Chavez's bullets, that the crime scene, the involvements, had expanded beyond control. He'd grabbed the tapes and taken off, the other two agents right behind. But once in the back alley, he heard the sirens and, knowing how deep in the shit he was, knew also the story could not fly. So he switched gears. He did something he would have bet would be harder but wasn't—he shot the two agents, close range, killing them.

Story: The Mayor and the Chief and the Director had asked him to infiltrate a squad of bigoted FBI agents by acting as their local liaison. The Mayor and the Chief, with the Director's blessing, enlisted Mallory to perform a sort of double-agent investigation. Because Mallory had been portrayed (unfairly, the Mayor himself pointed out) as a racist several times in city homicide cases, the bigoted agents accepted him. When the James boy turned up, Mallory went to his rescue. But he'd had to be careful, because he'd been outnumbered four to one at the house. However, when Long Ray made his move, Mallory saw the opportunity to break out of his double-agent status and help save the boy's life. This, the Mayor said, made him a true hero. The Director, the Mayor said, also deserved praise for his willingness to combat racism within the FBI.

Khalid's name never came up, the James boy never having seen him, Mallory keeping quiet about it.

Grandmother James, with the boy back, kept the media from him. She wanted to keep law enforcement from him, but the boy was insistent—he would talk. He would remember, and he would talk. Everything he knew, to anyone who would listen. And so what was on the tapes became public knowledge. Because the tapes were missing, the boy's statements could not be corroborated. But nonetheless, he told what he knew. He was afraid still. Showed it. Spoke anyway. His parents' child.

Long Ray was buried in the city's potter's field. He'd said years before that when he died he expected to be broke, but even if he wasn't, he wanted to be buried with all the city's other "poor-assed niggers."

Mrs. James brought the grandchildren to his funeral. Passer was there. Chavez. No one else.

Preacher was buried the same day as Long, in the same place. Mrs. James, the children, Passer, and Chavez were present for that too.

✳

Kellogg wasn't at the funeral because his condition was still too critical. He was now considered to be more likely to live than to die, but not much more likely.

"My fat saved my life," he tells Passer.

She says that's bullshit. He's just lucky—first, that the three bullets he took missed anything vital, and second, that Chavez's bullets didn't miss anything at all.

"So I'm a lucky man. Lucky to have so much unvital fat. But just in case my luck runs out, do me a favor. Contact my sisters and tell them what happened."

"What sisters?"

Kellogg sinks back into his hospital bed. Closes his eyes. Says, "Pass, why don't you pretend you've learned something these last two years and find them on your own. Let me sleep."

Mallory had snuck the videotapes away from the crime scene at Preacher's house. He made copies and delivered them to their respective cowards. To the Mayor and the FBI director, he said he wanted only backup on his story about the massacre. To Khalid, he said he wanted fifty thousand dollars, a number chosen because it would pay off the mortgage on his house in West Virginia.

Mallory goes to the hospital. Badges his way past the duty nurse telling him it's after visiting hours. Kellogg, hooked up to various monitors and fluids, is sleeping. Mallory sits by him, dozing off himself after a while. When he wakes, he finds Kellogg looking at him. The room is dark; the building quiet.

"What time is it?" Kellogg asks.

Mallory looks at his Rolex. "Two."

"A.M.?"

Mallory nods.

"Good time."

"You always liked it."

"Four A.M.'s better."

"A cop's time."

"Yeah."

Mallory holds up a package. Kellogg, from its shape, guesses. "A videotape?"

Mallory nods.

Kellogg guesses again, "Jimmy Close and Henry James in their 'historic' meeting?"

Mallory nods again. Says, "Wouldn't want you to die with a case hanging incomplete."

"You got the others too, then."

Mallory says nothing.

"Yeah, don't answer that," Kellogg says.

"Know what a house nigger is?" Mallory asks.

"Sure."

"A slave who lived in the big house with the white master, serving him, kissing his ass, sometimes making all the other slaves, the field niggers, jealous, but also sometimes being the one to get all the news to warn his people about what might be happening, sometimes able to stroke the master in just the right way to help his people."

"Uh-huh."

"That's me. According to the Mayor. I'm his house honky."

They laugh, Kellogg grimacing painfully as he does.

"You guys sure get along," Kellogg says.

"We think alike. I'll tell you something that most people wouldn't believe, but it's true—me and the Mayor might be the two least racist people you'll ever meet. Neither one of us cares about color."

"Neither one of you cares about anything except being in action."

"Exactly."

Mallory sets the wrapped tape on the bedstand. Asks, "How's your health?"

"Okay."

"Going to make it?"

"Probably."

"I was worried."

"Three bullets, I guess so."

"No, not that. Because with these borderline cases, it's usually the patient's will to live that makes the difference, and I wasn't sure you had any."

Kellogg smiles. "I'm surprised too."

"And speaking of will to live, shut that James boy up."

"I got nothing to do with that."

"I'm just saying he's asking for trouble."

"He's just telling the truth as he knows it. Fuck the world if it don't want to deal with the whole truth."

"All right. Don't matter, really. Nothing's coming of anything."

"No, you guys got it all worked out."

"So like I said, shut the kid up. What's the point in causing trouble? Especially racially?"

"It's kind of ironic that it's such an interracially harmonious cover-up."

"We *can* all just get along!"

They laugh.

"He's going to England anyway," Kellogg says. "The Jameses are."

"Good. It's probably a better country."

"Don't kid yourself."

"I mean racially."

"Me, too."

"Okay."

"We're just where the world's going."

"Okay."

"And speaking of where we're all going, if I do die, do me a favor."

Mallory touches the tape. "This ain't enough?"

"I'm going to tell you the same thing I told the Black Detective."

"What?"

"If Passer stays on, you guys treat her with all due respect."

"He told me you told him that."

"You guys talked?"

"Today. Talked good. Long time. He wanted to know the truth about everything. Promised to keep it to himself. Just wanted to know, you know. Killing curiosity."

"You told him?"

"Yeah. Like I said, we had a good long talk. Hell, we used to be friends."

"If I promise to keep my mouth shut, will you tell me everything?"

"As if you haven't figured it all out."

"I meant what I said about Passer."

"Black dick said you said she'd have made a great cop, except she's too afraid of violence."

"Not too afraid of it. Too saddened by it."

Mallory nods. Rises. Takes Kellogg's hand. Squeezes it. Says, "Yo, brother."

Kellogg nods.

Mallory leaves.

"Asshole!" Passer screams, slamming the door behind her as she enters the office.

Sue Cline, at her desk, jumps.

"I'm sorry, Sue. I didn't know you were here."

"I was just getting ready to go visit Kevin. Want to come?"

"I was just there."

"That explains the 'asshole.' He makes people talk like that."

"Did you know he has family?"

"I thought he might, but he wouldn't ever talk about it. I know his parents are dead."

"Well, he says he has sisters, but of course the *asshole* wouldn't tell me their names or where to find them."

She sits. Sighs deeply. Sue sees she's been crying.

"We're so scared for him, and he's so callous about our fears," Passer says.

"He's just being him."

"I know."

"Besides, maybe it's a compliment that he didn't give you his sisters' names. I mean, it's probably an easier find than a standard skip trace. Maybe he didn't want to insult you by suggesting you needed more information. It's a male

thing. Male mentor thing. I mean, he's still an asshole, but
. . . you know."

Passer does the work. It isn't hard, doesn't take long.
Finds the sisters, two of them, living together in Utah. She
gets one on the phone. Finds out they're both widowed.

The sister Passer talks to says they haven't heard from
Kevin for a long, long time. There was more than a ten-year
age gap, so they hadn't grown up close. But also there was a
specific falling-out. After their mother died in 1967, their
father having died earlier, the sisters wanted to sell the mod-
est family home there in D.C., which had been left to the
three of them. Kevin had talked them out of it. Then the
riots came in '68, and the last whites in the already changing
neighborhood left—were "driven out," the sister said. Now
the sisters got their way and the house was sold, but its value
had dropped even more. The split between them wasn't
about the money they had lost because Kevin made them
wait that extra year, though. It was about attitude, or stub-
bornness, or something. Anyway, the sisters kept sending
Kevin a card every Christmas, just to keep the door open
between them. But he never answered. The sister Passer
speaks to isn't surprised to hear he was shot. Living in Washington with "those people."

"Kevin's like a ghost to us now," she says. "So long lost.
It's like hearing from a ghost."

Khalid, without his entourage and dressed as middle class as
he can be, in slacks and sweater and nice shoes, not in his
New Africa uniform-suit, knocks on Mrs. James's door. After
a moment, she opens it. Stands there, not moving to invite
him in.

"Mrs. James?"

"Yes."

"I'm Khalid."

"I know who you are."

"I was a friend of your son's."

"I had two sons."

"Long."

"I know which one."

He nods. "I just wanted to tell you that Long . . ." Tears form in his eyes. He bows his head. "Long was the strongest man I've ever known. He was a great man. The absolute bravest man." He looks up at her. "I don't know how many times people have told you good things about him. Maybe no one ever has. But I wanted to. I wanted you to know that a lot of people looked up to him. I wanted you to know what a leader he was. It was in prison, but still, it's where he was, and he was the best. He kept the peace, there, better than anyone before or since. And that's something."

She nods, touched by Khalid's sincerity.

"I was just afraid that the only opinions on Long you ever heard came from cops or judges or probation officers or teachers. I wanted you to know what *we* thought of him. What I thought."

She nods again.

He takes a deep breath. Releases it. Wipes his eyes. Looks around. Feels better. "Is there anything you need? Anything I can do for you?"

"No."

"Security, maybe?"

"No."

"I hear you're moving to England."

She shakes her head. No.

He nods. Says, "Good."

"Yes."

"Peace."

"Yes. Peace."

He nods again. Turns. Goes down the steps to the street, to the city.

He goes for a long walk on this pretty evening. Through the great mix of people that is America. Wonders if it will be as costly for him as it was for Malcolm, to settle his anger, to grow his patience, to find his fairness, to understand his humanity, to rise above his hate of the hate, his fear of his fear. Wonders if he can do it. If anyone can. Flawed Malcolm, flawed Martin, flawed Lincoln, flawed Jefferson. He thinks of something Long said to him once, about how, when you're figuring out the cost of doing something, don't forget to consider the cost of not doing it, too. And when Khalid thinks of that, of Long, a wild rush of tears breaks from his eyes, as he stands there in the street, people staring.